Pinky Pye

Also by Eleanor Estes

GINGER PYE

THE WITCH FAMILY

THE MOFFATS

THE MIDDLE MOFFAT

RUFUS M.

THE MOFFAT MUSEUM

THE HUNDRED DRESSES

MIRANDA THE GREAT

Pinky Pye

Eleanor Estes

ILLUSTRATED BY
EDWARD ARDIZZONE

AN ODYSSEY/HARCOURT YOUNG CLASSIC
HARCOURT, INC.
SAN DIEGO NEW YORK LONDON

First Harcourt Young Classics edition 2000
First Odyssey Classics edition 2000
First published 1958

www.harcourt.com

Library of Congress Cataloging-in-Publication Data
Estes, Eleanor, 1906–
Pinky Pye/Eleanor Estes; illustrated by Edward Ardizzone.
p. cm.
"An Odyssey/Harcourt Young Classic."
Summary: While spending a bird-watching summer on Fire Island, the Pye family acquires a small black kitten that can use a typewriter.
[1. Cats—Fiction. 2. Family life—Fiction. 3. Fire Island (N.Y.)—Fiction.] I. Ardizzone, Edward, 1900– , ill. II. Title.
PZ7.E749Pi 2000
[Fic]—dc21 00-23879
ISBN 0-15-202559-6 ISBN 0-15-202565-0 (pb)

Printed in the United States of America

C E G H F D B
C E G H F D B (pb)

To Helena

CONTENTS

Pinky Pye

1

The Pyes Without Pinky

One day, guess who was standing on a little wharf in a town on Long Island waiting for a boat to carry them across the Great South Bay to another island named Fire Island. The Moffats? No. They never went away from Cranbury. The Pyes? Right. Ordinarily the Pyes never went away from Cranbury either, except for Papa, who was a renowned ornithologist and accustomed to travel in places near, faraway, and even dangerous. How did it happen then that all the Pyes—Mr. and Mrs. Pye, Jerry age ten, Rachel age nine, their small Uncle Bennie age three, their year-old smart dog Ginger, and Gracie, their eleven-year-old smart cat—amidst piles of luggage and parcels with strings hanging loose, signs of a long and wearying trip, were standing here on this briny-smelling wharf instead of being in their own tall house in Cranbury, Connecticut?

It happened that about a week ago Papa, who was the main person the senators and the representatives

in Washington depended upon for solving hard problems dealing with birds, had received a dispatch from these important men asking him to go to a place named Fire Island and make a study of the birds there, if he were interested, that is, they said courteously.

"A new journey so soon!" thought the Pyes. Papa had only just returned from a trip to the West Coast, where he had been comparing notes with another ornithologist, Mr. Hiram Bish, who, Papa said, owned the smallest owl he had ever seen, a baby pygmy owl. It wasn't more than two inches high, and it was the special pet of Mr. Hiram Bish and his wife. Papa might be a famous bird man, but he had never brought a bird home from his travels to keep for a pet as this other ornithologist had.

"Too many other pets in this house," he'd say with a shrug. "Supposing I studied bugs, would you want the house full of bugs?"

"No," was the swift reply.

The only bird that Papa had was a stuffed screech owl in his study, and this had been the gift of Mrs. Moffat, who had donated it to him when she had moved from the Yellow House on New Dollar Street, because, in her new and smaller house on Ashbellows Place, she had no attic and no room for stuffed screech owls.

Usually Papa's bird studies led him to faraway places, the Everglades, the barren lands of Labrador, and, once, South America. Of course Papa had never been able to take his family with him to these far and dangerous places even though Rachel, up until the very moment of his departure, hoped he would invite at least her, for she planned to be an ornithologist herself someday. But Papa did not know about this plan, and he always gave her an absentminded kiss and hug, the same as he did everybody else in the family. "Be sure and lock the cellar door each night," he'd say. It was as though this remark was his way of saying, "Take good care of yourselves." And then off he would go, lugging his suitcase to the corner of Elm Street where the trolley ran.

In view of these far places to which Papa usually went, it was a great surprise, then, when the men in Washington wrote and suggested that he go to Fire Island, which was really quite near. The reason the men in Washington asked Papa to go to Fire Island was that they wanted to print a document about the birds there and they felt that Pye was the man for the job. An inhabitant of the island, one of the few all-year-round inhabitants, not a bird spotter or anything of that sort, just a regular inhabitant—her name was Mrs. A. A. Pulie—had discovered a puffin there. Bird spotter or not, Mrs. Pulie, having spent her entire life on this island, had plenty of sense about what birds you were supposed to see there and what you weren't, and she knew that a puffin was out of the ordinary. So she had reported it to the Bureau of Birds, which had promised an investigation, it was that curious about the puffin. And, in her turn, Mrs. Pulie had offered to rent her cottage to the ornithologist of Washington's choosing, at a very modest rental, *she* was that curious about the puffin and birds in general.

Fire Island is a long and skinny island just south of Long Island, which is also a long and skinny island, though it is fatter than Fire Island and much longer. If Long Island had not been in the Sound just south of Connecticut, you might have been able to see Fire Island from Cranbury, town of the Pyes and Moffats. Probably not. But who knows? On a clear and sparkling day, who knows how far one sees?

When Papa had received the letter about Fire Island from the men in Washington, he said that if his check from *The Auk*, one of the learned magazines for which he wrote, came on time (for the men in Washington said nothing about paying for the expenses; they just said wouldn't it be nice to find out about the puffin and the Fire Island birds?), he would pack up the entire family and take them along with him on this near and pleasant bird expedition. They could stay for the entire summer, he said, smiling his nice sideways smile.

The check from *The Auk* had come, on time. "Hurray!" said Papa. "We can go! We can spend the whole summer. I can write ten books!" he said. Papa was always about ten books behind in his writing.

Rachel and Jerry had happened to be sitting on the little upstairs porch when they heard this astonishing news. At first they did not know whether to be happy or sad, for they had never before been away from Cranbury for that long a time. "What! The whole summer!" they said to each other. "Go to Fire Island for the whole summer!" It sounded like the hottest place outside of the sun that they had ever heard of, excellent for winter expeditions perhaps, but . . . go to Fire Island for the whole summer! Just throw away the whole wonderful summer in Cranbury when there was no school and no Sunday school, only church to go to? They had a beach here, didn't they? Sandy Beach, dear Sandy Beach. Why go to another beach just because it had a different name? And they had woods here, didn't they, and brooks and fields and daisies and summer, long and wonderful summer. Just throw it all away, waste it. It would be like skipping a chapter in a book; or like having a chapter, the best one probably in the whole book, either torn out or so blurrily printed it could not be read.

"The Moffats never go away," said Rachel.

"No. Neither do most people," said Jerry.

"No. They sit on their porches and rock in the evenings, and they hose their lawns."

Here in Cranbury it was nice. On misty days it smelled like the sea, for it was near the sea. And after a thunderstorm the town smelled particularly wonderful. The gutters gurgled merrily then with the swift rainwater racing to the drains, with sticks for boats and chewing-gum papers for rafts bumping into each other as they were swirled along. A person could go barefoot in the wet and new-cut grass.

Then Rachel hit herself hard on the head. "Am I crazy?" she asked herself. "Look at me! A girl who at last has a chance to go with a famous father on a famous expedition to watch birds and what does she do? She wishes she could stay home in Cranbury, same old Cranbury. Am I a nut?" she asked herself scornfully. "No," came the answer quickly. "I'm really happy to be going. I'm going to be a bird man too someday, and this may be the beginning. I may be the one to discover an important discovery. About a feather, at least, if not the whole bird."

Rachel waited tensely for what Jerry would say next. She liked life best when she and Jerry thought exactly the same about things, unless they were playing a game, of course. Then she would have to take an opposite side or where would the game be? When Jerry's reaction did come, it was strong.

"What!" he squealed when he was certain that Papa was way up in his study, his Eyrie, as it was called, and could not hear him. "What! Not go up to the woods and the resevoy every minute and catch frogs and cook them and eat them, and everything, with Dick and his big dog Duke and me with my dog Ginger! O-o-oh!" he groaned.

Then he fell silent, and Rachel wondered if she would have to go back to not wanting to go too since he didn't and this wasn't a game calling for opposite sides. But then Jerry said, "Well, you know what? There are breakers there. It is like Hawaii, and you can coast in on a breaker. I've seen breakers in moving pictures, colored pictures, and you roll in, in Waikiki."

"Oh, yes," thrilled Rachel.

"Besides, I may find some ancient specimen of rock, some unusual specimen, not a Cranbury or a Sleeping Giant one but an unusual one, a million years old."

Specimens were what Jerry was interested in, not birds that fly away before one can be sure what they are but specimens of rock that may be scrutinized at leisure in one's room by lamplight, late. Rocks were always tumbling out of his pockets, wearing holes in them. He loved rocks. He didn't know whether there were any rocks on Fire Island or not, but whoever heard of any place, except perhaps the desert, without some rock?

"Probably Fire Island was named Fire Island because when the earth broke away from the sun, probably that part cooled last," he said to Rachel, who nodded understandingly and admired this display of scientific knowledge. She secretly vowed to read *Popular Mechanics* from A to Z as her brother did so she would know *something*.

"It's probably all just plain hot rock, cold now though," she suggested, hoping the latter was the case.

Papa had been too excited and happy to stay up in his study and work. After all, this was the first all-summer-long vacation he had ever taken his family on, and naturally he was pleased. He joined Jerry and Rachel on the little square porch.

"I suppose we'll have to take Ginger somehow or another," he said.

"Ginger," said Jerry, "did you know that you are going on a trip?"

Ginger wagged his tail and leaped up ready to go.

Ginger was known throughout Cranbury as "the intellectual dog" because once he had found one of Jerry's pencils, tracked Jerry to school, and gone up the fire escape with it to Jerry's very classroom. Of course they had to take him. Moreover, he had been lost from Thanksgiving Day until the twenty-ninth of May! Rachel and Jerry had only just been reunited with him. They couldn't part with him again, leave him behind. Someone might steal him again, such a smart dog. The Pyes could not take a chance like that. And besides, imagine Ginger's eyes when he saw that he was being left, the awful look in his sad eyes!

"Yes," said Papa. "Bring Ginger, of course. But not Gracie. Gracie cannot come."

"What!" exclaimed Mama, who was running the mop around the upstairs hall and hearing every word they said. "What! Not bring Gracie!"

"No," said Papa. "I can't have that cat chasing away the few birds there are on that island. She can stay with Gramma."

Mama shook her head firmly and banged the mop against the banister. "She's got to come," she said. Gracie had been a wedding present to Mama and Papa, and she was known all over town as "the New York cat."

"Gracie would pine away," said Mama. "She would miss me so. I've heard of cats just pining away." The way she said "pining" brought tears to Rachel's eyes, though she was not very fond of the fabulous New York cat, who had an unpleasant habit of fixing her eyes on Rachel with a green and glassy stare.

"I'll keep Gracie away from you and your birds," said Mama. "After all, with that bell around her neck she doesn't even try to bother the birds here, so why should she bother the birds there? She won't. She can't. In fact, she is a good spotter, and she may lead you to some bird whose existence there you would not otherwise suspect. Not another puffin perhaps, but some bird equally unique."

So Papa said all right, let Gracie come too. Gracie was sitting on the high banister and she surveyed them all coldly and indifferently. "And let Uncle Bennie come too if he can," said Papa.

At first Uncle Bennie's mother did not want him to go. A whole summer seemed like such an awfully long time to be parted from him. But since he was looking pale, having just had the chicken pox, she finally said, "All right."

After all, Uncle Bennie would be with Mrs. Pye, who was his own big sister, which made him the uncle of Jerry and Rachel, though he was not half as old. He was only three, and he had been born an uncle. Some people are never uncles, but he had been one from the start, ever since he was a minute old; a minute-old uncle is what he had once been.

Since his mother still looked sad at the idea of the long separation, Uncle Bennie said to her, "If the fire's too hot on that island that's on fire, I'll come back. I'll swim back. I can swim, you know," he said indignantly, though so far no one had said he couldn't. "On the bottom of the bath tub, I swim."

It was fortunate that Uncle Bennie had no large pets to bring with him, for how to transport Gracie and Ginger was going to be a great problem. But all Uncle Bennie had in the way of pets was a dead locust on a string. This dead locust slept on a little bed Uncle Bennie had patted down for him of pieces of cloth in a light yellow Coats' thread box. He had punched holes in the lid of the box for his pet. "What are those for?" asked Jerry.

"For him to breathe. Some dead things do breathe, you know," said Uncle Bennie.

Then the packing in both houses had begun.

"We might as well take every piece of clothing we own, being gone that long," said Mama.

"Even leggin's?" asked Rachel.

"Well . . . I suppose not leggings," said Mama hesitantly, for leggings were a tempting idea. The island sounded hot, but should one judge by names? Consider Iceland and Greenland, each one being just the opposite of what it sounded like, according to the geographies.

Mama would pack a valise and then unpack it again, thinking some garment was at the bottom that should be at the top. Sweaters should certainly be at the top, where they could be reached in a hurry. The children might start off thinly clad for a hot day and then the weather might suddenly turn cold. What is worse than being cold and shivering and having everyone start the summer with a cold? And no doctors there. Perhaps not even a drugstore there with a wonderful druggist like their own Dr. Sheppard, who could tell you what the doctor was likely to prescribe, thus saving you a great deal of money.

No. Packing had not been as simple as it sounded, especially with Miss Lamb at the library urging Rachel and Jerry to take eight more books every time they went in. There were so many books by authors whose names began with an *A* or a *B* they had to be piled on the floor and on the windowsills.

"Here's a good book," she'd say because it wouldn't fit in the *A*s or *B*s. And they'd take it.

"If only," the Pyes thought over and over again as the hard job of packing went on, "we were either there on Fire Island or here and all nicely unpacked and things put away and us settled in our lives as we used to be!"

Fortunately their important High School Senior friend, Sam Doody, the captain of the team and the greatest Boy Scout in Cranbury (he had once saved a life), had offered to drive the family and their pets dead and alive to the town on Long Island from which the boat sailed to Fire Island. Mama had been delighted, and it no longer mattered what she put on top in the suitcases or on the bottom or whether things stuck out of the sides. Nothing mattered since they were not going by train, and she had got out still more things to take, *War and Peace,* for instance, which she hoped this summer to finish. Last summer she had got up to page thirty-nine.

None of them had been in Sam Doody's present car. It was an old car but new to Sam. It was a touring car, a Model-T Ford touring car, and the black canvas top rolled back. Think of the air and sunshine in that, if you want!

At first Rachel had been disappointed not to be going on the train. She had really hoped to sleep on the train, look out of the window in the morning early, view the passing scene while eating a piece of toast. Suppose she saw the reservoir like that, they whizzing by it, she with a piece of toast!

But when she'd heard they would go by way of the Boston Post Road, she was not as disappointed. She had never been on this famous road, and she thought she'd see horses posting along delivering the post. "Giddyap-giddyap," she murmured.

"And now I can take more dolls," she had said happily, "since we are going in a car on the Boston Post Road." And she had tucked in another old doll, named Lydia, and a bagful of Lydia's clothes.

Right now then, as the family stood waiting for the boat to come, Lydia, with eyes as liquid as the blue sky above the bay, looked up expectantly at Rachel from the crate on which she lay sprawling.

Rachel stooped down and whispered in Lydia's ear. "Are you glad you came? We're about to set sail. Isn't that wonderful?"

2

The Eyrie

So there they stood then, all the Pyes, Ginger, rasping and gasping on his leash, Gracie, meowing inside her cardboard carton, Lydia, the blue-eyed doll, gazing happily up at the blue sky, all of them on the little wharf looking out over the Great South Bay, its ripples smooth and serene, a soothing balm to the tired nerves of the travelers. Packing was behind them, the Boston Post Road was behind them. Rachel had not even known they were on the Boston Post Road until they were off it. Not a horse came posting by. No coaches. One ice wagon and several moving vans drawn by horses—that was all there was in the horse line. It was an ugly road with thousands of signs on it. ENNA JETTICK, said many of these signs. Enna Jettick was not a lady, it was a shoe.

Behind them, too, were countless flat tires. Fortunately some of these had occurred in pleasant spots. One had occurred near the Southport Railroad Station, where, longingly, the children watched the trains streak by as Sam and Papa changed the tire of their Model-T Ford. You might think that Papa, being mainly a bird man, would not be handy with a jack and a wrench. But he was handy, and he could, moreover, crank up the car and make it heave and shake and get ready to go.

And behind them was the wearying but extraordinary ride through New York City, where the children hoped for a glimpse at least—if not a run up it too—of the famous escalator where once, running up the down one, Papa had bumped into Mama. And finally, behind them was the speedy journey, hitting sometimes thirty-two miles an hour ("Don't go so fast! Don't go so fast!" Mama would beg, for she hated speed), out of the city and down the island to this little wharf.

Now. Ahead lay the Great South Bay cupped in the golden arms of sunset, a ride across it in a boat, and then—Fire Island! Fire Island and a whole long summer in a little cottage called The Eyrie.

Rachel and Jerry thought that it was an exceptional happening for Papa not only to have a study at home called the Eyrie, but also to have rented a cottage with the same identical name. How many eyries are there in the world that the Pyes should be connected with two of them?

They turned from the bay a moment to wave to Sam Doody, who gave them a last cheerful wave with his pipe and a toot of his horn as he drove off the dock and started on his long and lonesome ride home. How empty his car was now! He swung one long lanky leg over the door. *That Sam!* they thought fondly. *Showing off!* Then, shielding their eyes from the crimson setting sun, they peered across the bay for their boat, which, they had learned from a man with a can full of worms, was called the *Maid of the Bay.* They supposed this boat would at least be as big as the *Richard Peck,* a boat that sailed back and forth from New Haven to New York that they had all been on once.

Right below them a little launch was moored. "Glub, glub," it said complacently as it bobbed in the waves. Looking down at it for the first time, they saw its name. "The *Maid of the Bay*!" they exclaimed.

Though it was little, it was a sturdy boat. A man in faded blue pants was sitting in the stern, smoking a pipe and looking up at them. It was rather disconcerting for the Pyes to realize that somebody had been observing them without their being aware of it, and they hoped they had said nothing stupid. They were going to a new place and did not want to start off seeming stupid.

The man said, not giving a sign as to whether he thought they were stupid or not, "Don't you want to load up?"

"Yes, yes," they all said. They answered quickly, the way people answer in New York, where the quickest and least stupid people in the world live, according to Mama. They hoped to counteract the bad impression they may have made on the man by looking for the *Maid of the Bay* out at sea when here she had been all along right under their noses. Rachel wished she had said, "Aye, aye, sir," for she knew it was correct to say "Aye, aye, sir" to sailors and "Ah, men" to God.

"I wonder if we are the only people going over there," said Mama. And, "Is this boat safe?" she whispered to Papa.

"Very," he answered.

"I like land that is joined to land, not separated," said Mama, but she said it to herself, not to cast a gloom. Really the only islands she liked were the little ones in the sound that they waded to when the tide was low, ate their picnics on, and then waded away from and back to the mainland before the tide came in again. *Well,* she thought. *This island is not* very *far, though too far for wading.* And out loud she said, "Well, come on, let's get in the boat."

It was lucky there were no other passengers. The Pyes and their luggage took up most of the space. Mama let Gracie out of her box to take in the situa-

tion and to stretch her legs. She looked over the side of the boat in astonishment, drew back, and then looked again, long-neckedly, fascinated though terrified. Ginger was leaning over the side so far that his nose got wet in the salt spray, and he kept licking it eagerly. Papa picked up a newspaper that someone had left on the boat, and he tucked it in his pocket to read later.

Looking toward their destination, Uncle Bennie said, "Is that the island we're going to?"

"Yes," said Papa.

"Well, it is on fire," said Uncle Bennie happily.

"That's sunset all over the sky," said Rachel. "Not fire."

They were putting busily along, and smoothly, and everyone was enjoying the cool ride. What a relief after the Model-T touring car with its loud bangs and its flat tires and black canvas top that kept flying up unexpectedly. How cozy it was in this little boat! How cool! They could sail on and on and on. Fishermen in large and small boats were coming home, gulls screaming behind them, protesting, quarreling.

"Smell the air!" they said. "Oh, smell it!" The boat ride was a wonderful start to what must be going to be a great and beautiful summer.

It took about a half hour to cross the bay. Then the boat pulled alongside a sturdy dock, and the minute the Pyes stepped off they took in, in one glance, the fact that this place had an unusually inviting feeling to it. Half a dozen small boys were being extremely active and noisy, all leaning over the side of the dock, practically grabbing at the Pyes and their luggage.

"Wagon! Wagon!" they called, each one trying to push in first.

No cars were allowed on this island, nothing on wheels in fact, except bicycles and small boys' express wagons. These small boys ran the only taxicab business there was, hauling people's luggage in their wagons, charging ten cents a load.

"Wagon! Wagon!" they yelled instead of "Taxi! Taxi!" One said, "Smash yer baggage?"

He must be a New York boy, thought Rachel. *He talks like a boy in an Alger book.*

An alert boy of about nine, whose face was covered with a white powder ("For poison ivery," he explained), took their bags and tied them on his excellent long and flat and homemade wagon. (*I'm going to make one just like that,* thought Jerry, *and join the taxi business.*) Naturally, everything would not fit on this one boy's taxi, and in the end, even though it cost sixty cents, Papa had to employ every boy in sight. Besides this, each member of the family had to carry many things.

"Don't lose anything," cautioned Mama, who was half smothered under the pile of coats and sweaters that had been shed, one by one, as they had progressed along the Boston Post Road. All in all, it was quite a long caravan that started down the narrow boardwalk toward the ocean.

Just as there were no vehicles on this island, so there were no streets either. There were very narrow boardwalks instead, and people had to walk single file, Indian fashion. The first boy, with the poison ivy, whose name turned out to be Touhy Tomlinson, said there were six of these lanes crossing the island, which was only a quarter of a mile wide from bay to ocean. And there were three lanes going the long way of the narrow island.

"Do you know where The Eyrie is?" asked Papa.

"Oh, yes," said Touhy, and the caravan proceeded.

Uncle Bennie, being very tired, sat on top of wagon one and tried to count the number of different rides he had had that day. Losing track, he comfortably sucked his thumb and felt in his pocket for a shred of old blanket he called "Bubbah," with which he liked to tickle his nose as he sucked his thumb. "Just nine more days. Just nine more days," he chanted. He was referring to the time left for the pleasure of thumb sucking that he was going to give up on the Fourth of July, which happened also to be his birthday. Sam Doody had said to him, "Who ever heard of a boy of four sucking his thumb?" So of course he had to give it up.

On their way to the little house they saw a great deal of poison ivy. "It is the chief crop here," said Touhy Tomlinson.

Most of the trees were twisted little scrub pines with a few hollies mixed in. Between the cottages, knobby clumps of tall tough grass grew, and over some of the cottages pale pink roses bloomed. All the houses looked inviting.

"You know what this place looks like?" said Rachel. "It looks like a toy village. You know Joey Moffat? He has a toy village, and these houses set out in straight little rows look like his village."

"Well," said Uncle Bennie, who also knew Joey's village, "where's the milk wagon here? And the bakery wagon?" He paused a moment. Then he said, "I wish I was home. I wish I never came. What's that roar?"

"That's the ocean," said Mama. "It's the sound of the surf, and it will put us to sleep every night."

"Not innerested," said Uncle Bennie gloomily.

A short way ahead, on a slight rise so that it was a little higher than the others, Rachel could see a perfect little brown-shingled, weather-beaten cottage. Could it be The Eyrie? It looked like a dollhouse. Many of the houses were like rectangular boxes. But this one had corners and elbows to it as though a room or a porch had been added here or there as an afterthought. Very pale pink roses spread sparsely over the tiny porch roof. The baggage boys slowed up. Everyone got a good view of the front of the cottage.

THE EYRIE, said the sign over the door.

All the Pyes were enchanted, and Uncle Bennie cheered up too. It was a perfect house in which to spend a summer. Stepping inside, almost expecting to discover the three bears in a little house like this, they found, not bears, but other surprises—little alcoves, built-in tables on which to work or eat or study or play Canfield, and one was set for supper.

Someone knocked lightly at the door. Astonished at having a caller when they had just barely arrived, the Pyes all rushed to open it. The caller was Mrs. A. A. Pulie, discoverer of the puffin and owner of the cottage. She had a trowel in her hands. *Been digging clams,* thought Uncle Bennie.

"Ah, Mrs. Pulie?" said Papa.

"Yes," said this sunburned, leathery-faced lady. "And you, of course, are Mr. Pye, the famous ornithologist, Mr. Edgar Pye."

Papa lowered his eyes. He was not accustomed to people knowing, or at least saying, that he was famous. He hardly knew it himself, and it battened him down to have someone come right out like this and say it in front of everybody.

The boys had not yet been paid their dimes, and they were standing by with their poison-ivy faces impassive and unimpressed by fame. Papa paid them and they left. The lady continued.

"It is an honor," she said, "for me to rent my cottage to such a distinguished gentleman. I, too, am a birdaceous creature, birdaceous and boldaceous, both. I imagine this will be a real vacation for you." She laughed gaily. "Few birds here to speak of aside from the terns—the large and the lesser terns."

It sounds like an English lesson, thought Rachel, wondering if there were a least tern too.

"And the puffin, wherever it is," Mrs. Pulie went on. "Anyway, since you are a noted ornithologist, Mr. Pye, who knows what surprises the birds of our island may have in store for you?" Then she said, "Well, I know you are all tired. And hungry. So I'll go now and leave you alone. I know you will enjoy The Eyrie. I had it built and I have loved it. Now I am building a larger cottage farther down the beach."

Oh, thought Uncle Bennie. *Digging cellars. Not clams.*

"Mrs. Pulie," said Rachel shyly. "Why did you call this cottage The Eyrie?"

"Because this cottage is just a little higher than any other cottage. And because I have always loved words pertaining to birds. I am naming my new cottage The Gullery, you see, like *scullery* only *gullery*. A word I coined."

"Oh," said Rachel.

Mrs. Pulie then explained about the kerosene stove, the fireplace, the icebox—"not to forget to empty the water under it"—her unusual mailbox, and the little alcove under the eaves.

"I've left a few of my things up in the eaves. I

hope you don't mind." "Up in the eaves" was the way Mrs. Pulie referred to the dark little alcove high up under the roof of The Eyrie, and from then on that was how the Pyes referred to that important section.

When Mrs. Pulie left, the Pyes busily and happily explored the cottage. There were benches that opened up under windows where toys could be kept. There were a few little spiders in these but not many, and in one they found some toys left by some other child from some other year and a waterstained book about missionaries. Then the door opened again and Mrs. Pulie came back in. "I forgot to tell you," she said. "There's a little window, a sort of round porthole window up in the eaves, which I opened this morning in order to air out the cottage. After a while you better close it so it won't rain in. You have to get up to the eaves either by stepladder from the inside, or by climbing up on the roof of the porch on the outside."

"All right. We'll remember," promised Papa, absently and forgetting about it immediately. After all, he had a great deal on his mind—birds, family, the end of the trip, getting ice in, getting food in, the beds made up. Not only Papa forgot; everyone else forgot, too, about the little porthole window that Mrs. Pulie said to be sure to close.

"Good-bye. Good-bye," they said to her. They liked her and they wished she would not go. In the dim light of the kerosene lamp it seemed lonesome without the lady, to be here on this island in this cottage with the lady gone and the boat gone too, and also the wagon boys; and to have just a handful of cottages that had lights on in them scattered here and there. In Cranbury there was a lighted-up house every minute, and you could hear the trains and trolleys, the sound of voices and the singing of crickets.

Suddenly they became aware of a high and shrill and desperate sound that went on and on without pause. It was not a ringing in the ears as Rachel had first thought.

"Peepers," said Papa. "Just peepers."

"Peepers!" exclaimed Jerry. "There must be a million of them to make all that noise!"

Papa spread out the newspaper he had picked up on the boat. Naturally he didn't have time to read it this minute, but he did want to glance at the headlines. "Why, here's a funny thing," he said. "You remember my friend Hiram Bish, out West? That fellow with the little owl. Well, it says here in the paper that he is on his way east right now with that little owl. He's coming by boat, through the canal, on the SS *Pennsylvania.* Here's a picture of the little owl."

Everyone crowded around Papa. "Newcomer on way to zoo," said the headline. The owl looked very disgruntled in the picture, indignant.

"O-o-oh," murmured Rachel. "Isn't he cute!"

She clipped the story out of the paper because she was going to keep a scrapbook of unusual stories about birds this summer, and this would be the first one in it.

After a quick supper of alphabet soup they went to bed. This house was so little they could talk to one another without yelling from one room to the next, right from their beds. Uncle Bennie was sleeping on a cot in Rachel's little room because, of all the Pyes, he was the fondest of her. His pet, the dead locust, was in its box under his cot. "Sleep," Uncle Bennie said to it. Jerry was sleeping on a cot on the small glass-enclosed porch off the living room. Papa and Mama were in the other bedroom. Ginger was allowed to sleep where he always slept, and this, of course, was on Jerry's feet. Gracie slept where she wanted, and this was on Mama's feet.

A gull, out late, came screaming by. "Oh, remind me," said Papa, "to close that little window up in the eaves tomorrow."

"All right," said Mama. She yawned sleepily. "We certainly don't want any bats or things flying in there."

One by one, to the music of the surf and the peepers, they all fell asleep.

3

Abandoned!

On the first morning of the Pyes' stay on Fire Island, they waked up in the wonderful way they were going to wake up practically every morning there—sun shining brightly through the windows on the ocean side, waves booming and breaking down below, gulls screaming over on the bay side about the fish business.

First, before breakfast even, the children decided to do some exploring. Probably Mama would not let them go swimming, for it was an old rule of the Pye household that no one could go in swimming until the Fourth of July. However, since they were not in Cranbury, since they were here in new territory, Jerry and Rachel decided to test the old Fourth-of-July rule. "May we go in swimming?" they said to Mama.

The same old rule did prevail. "No," said Mama. "Not today. Not until the Fourth of July."

"But it's hot," they said.

"Not that hot," said Mama. She wetted her finger like an Indian or a Boy Scout and held it up to the wind. "See, there's a wind," she said. "Besides, Papa or I must be with you when you swim in the ocean. You may swim in the bay without us. Not Uncle Bennie; but you may."

The children didn't really care. It was wonderful here. There wasn't a cloud in the sky. They bet it never rained here. They rolled down the high dune to the beach. "Smell it!" they kept exclaiming as they trudged along. And, "Hey, taste your arm!" They tasted their arms, and their arms tasted like the salt sea. They hadn't even been in swimming and still they tasted like the sea. Uncle Bennie's thumb would taste better than ever, and it would be doubly hard for him to give up sucking it forevermore on the Fourth of July.

"I don't care," he muttered to himself. "I give up my thumb and I go swimming instead. That's fair, isn't it?"

They climbed back up the dune, not the easy way by the wooden stairs, but the hard way, up the slippery sand dune. They walked along the top of the dune and watched the ocean come rolling, roaring in down below. A ship was on the horizon. Papa had said they would be able to see the great ocean liners in the distance, the *Mauretania* or the *Minnetonka.* The children thought they might see the very boat on which Mr. and Mrs. Hiram Bish were, at this very moment, traveling with their little owl, their final destination being the Washington zoo. They didn't know that this would be a little off the course of boats from the West Coast. They hadn't been here very long and didn't know everything yet.

"Why, it's as though we've been here forever. We even know people," said Rachel. "There's Mrs. Pulie. There she goes."

"I know it," said Jerry. "See those boys over there? I know them all."

These were the wagon boys on their way to meet the morning boat and to hang around the wharf. "Hi!" they yelled to Jerry.

"See! I have friends," said Jerry. "Hi, Touhy," he called nonchalantly.

They sauntered up one narrow boardwalk and down another and they speedily determined which cottages had a boy or a girl in them. This was not hard because there would be a wagon in front of the house or a wet bathing suit on the line. All other households did not have the same Fourth-of-July swimming rule theirs did apparently.

And then they started for home. They knew what was poison ivy and they stayed out of it. "See that? That's poison ivery," said Uncle Bennie in regard to every single plant he saw, even plain pepper grass. There would be no chance of his getting poison ivy

because he was not going to step on any plant at all. That was what he had decided.

At home, breakfast was waiting for them. Just as each one hungrily took his first bite of pancake there came certain unusual noises from the front stoop. There were faint mews. But Gracie was on the mantel smelling old seaweed. And then there were frantic-sounding thrashings and beatings-about of something. Mama got the broom, and they all went to the front door. There, on the stoop, tangled in an old torn crab net, was a tiny skinny black kitten looking furious and bewildered. She had a string tied around her neck with a sign on it.

A BANDID, said the sign.

"A bandid?" said Rachel. "Must mean bandit. A bandit."

Everybody laughed at this idea, and the kitten, trying desperately to get loose, spat at them all.

"Abandoned!" said Papa, who was excellent at riddles. "That's what this sign means. Abandoned."

"An abandoned kitten!" they exclaimed compassionately.

"Is there anything else on the note?" asked Jerry, and, turning it over, he saw that there was. "My name is Pinky," he read, and, "I don't know how old is I."

"Oh, isn't it cunning?" said Rachel. "It is like in books. People abandon a kitten or a baby in a church pew or at some kind person's doorstep, hoping he will give it a home."

"I wish they had thought of church this time," said Mama wistfully.

Papa was gently untangling the kitten from the net. The kitten was crying so loudly its mouth was as wide open as a baby bird's. Why the kitten was named Pinky was a mystery, for it was mainly black with the exception of one pure white paw and a white nose with a comical black spot just off center. At last, clawing, scratching, biting, and hissing, the wispy little ball of fur was disengaged from the crab net. She faced them all with her A BANDID sign on her, arched her back, flattened down her ears, and challenged the entire group of them—people, dog, and cat. Suspecting that she would soon make a dash for freedom, Papa scooped her up in his hands.

Ginger whined. He wanted to chase her. "The poor little thing!" said Jerry. "Aren't you ashamed!"

Meanwhile, they all had a feeling that someone else was around—a person. When the children had returned from their walk just a few minutes ago, no one, no cat, nothing had been on the little front stoop. But the kitten, abandoned as she had been, must have been abandoned by someone. She could not have written the note around her neck herself, could she? Or hobbled there in her net? The Pyes listened. Saying nothing, keeping very quiet, their patience was rewarded, their suspicions proven correct. A little red-haired girl stuck her head around the corner of the house. Seeing that she had been observed, she withdrew it immediately. However, she couldn't resist, after a moment, sticking her head out again, as though to make sure of what she'd seen, and then quickly withdrawing it.

"Come here," demanded Papa.

The girl remained hidden, or perhaps she had run away. "Now you just come right here," said Papa kindly but firmly. And the girl came out. She had another crab net in her hands, and it was full of squirming, struggling kittens. "Yours is the prettiest," said the little girl. She looked to be about seven years old.

"Ours!" said Mama.

"Take it," said the girl. "Their mother was abandid by summer people last year. And now their mother has abandid them, or is lost. I caught them in a crab net this morning."

"Do you mean to say that summer people abandon their pets at the end of the season?" demanded Papa.

"That's right," said the girl, whose name was Rose.

"Oh, no!" said all the Pyes. "Abandoned!"

"Why don't you keep the kittens since you caught them?" suggested Mama.

"We already have nine abandid kittens, and my mother says that is all."

"Anyway," said Papa, speaking up firmly, "we are keeping this abandid kitten. I like her."

Everyone looked at Papa in amazement. Never on his bird travels had he brought home a bird. Now here he was on a bird expedition and adopting a kitten! The kitten, Pinky, looked up at him narrowly. The bristles on her back were going down. "We'll keep her," said Papa, "if you will promise to put bells on all your nine cats. That is to preserve our bird life," he explained to Rose, who seemed puzzled.

"Imagine bells on nine cats! *Ts, ts.* Rose's poor mother!" said Mama.

"Jingle bells, jingle bells," sang Uncle Bennie.

Papa had seen to it that practically all the cats in Cranbury had bells on them, and now, here he was, agitating for bells on all the cats here! *Well, no wonder,* thought Rachel. *He has to have some birds to study.*

"How did she get the name of Pinky?" she asked Rose.

"Because she has such a pink little tongue."

"Oh, of course."

"Could I have my sign back now?" said the little girl, for the deal seemed to be closed.

"Oh, couldn't we keep it for Pinky's scrapbook, her baby book?" asked Rachel. Rachel was a great keeper of scrapbooks and even had them for all her dolls.

"Well, all right," said Rose. "I'll make another one." And off she went with her sackful of kittens, to leave them, one by one, on other inviting doorsteps.

Mama said weakly, "We already have one cat, Gracie."

"Now we have two," said Papa firmly. And Pinky spat at Mama. "Ah, she's a little wild," said Papa fondly. "But with love and good food she will be a wonderful pet."

"Well," said Mama, a soft look coming over her

face. "The poor abandoned little thing. If we don't take her, who knows what awful person might and keep her just for the summer and then—abandon her again. Maybe we should take them all," she said, compassion overriding her common sense.

"One is plenty," said Papa.

"Woe," said Pinky, for that was the way she said "mew."

"Ah-h," said Uncle Bennie, "a baby."

Rachel asked to hold her. She pressed the tiny kitten, which seemed to weigh nothing, against her cheek. "Oh, you cunning little thing!" she said. Pinky gave her first purr. She did it again, looking as astonished as the Pyes at her unusually loud and enginelike noises. Her whole skinny little body shook. These purrs may have been the first ones of her life.

For the next two hours Rachel sat in a little rocking chair holding the kitten. She rocked her and rocked her, and she sang softly to her. Tired from her adventures and travels and having only this morning been torn asunder from her life in the reeds and rushes, Pinky fell asleep, her little pointed face resting in the palm of Rachel's hand.

Gracie pretended not to notice this scene. Whenever she came in the living room, she skirted the edges, hitched her shoulders, sat down on the hearth, and shook her front paw as though she had stepped in mud. As the day went on, Gracie wore a smug smile on her face. Once she came up to Pinky and gave her a patronizing sniff. Then she gave Pinky a little lick and hastened away as though ashamed of her sentimentality. Gracie had often been a mother long ago, and possibly Pinky aroused her old feelings of mother love.

After a while Pinky gave a little yawn showing her raspberry-colored tongue. It looked as soft as a rose petal, but it felt as rough as a thistle. And at this moment Ginger, who had spent these two hours with Jerry and the wagon boys, rushed in to have a drink. He drew back in surprise when he saw Pinky. Apparently he had thought she'd be gone by now. And the sudden sight of Ginger interrupted Pinky in the middle of a stretch. She just kept her back up and arched it to its capacity. Ginger barked. Pinky spat. She was not the least afraid, and the fact that Ginger was the worst chaser of cats in all of Cranbury would have made no difference to her even if she had known it.

Pinky had not spent her early weeks in the jungle of sea grass and marsh for nothing, living by her wits and cleverness. She had no intention of running away. Continuing to arch her bony back, she hissed again and again, like a snake. She stiffened all her fur, and you could almost count the hairs, they stood out so. She was puny, but she was full of dynamite.

Rachel couldn't hold her. She jumped down and she leaped toward Ginger as if on springs, sideways, all four legs going up in the air at once in the manner of certain mountain goats. Spitting and hissing, she came in her sideways leaps. Her ears were pasted down, her blue eyes were black.

She slapped at Ginger and then she raced for the couch and dived under it. While Ginger sniffed and barked at the place in the middle of the couch where she had disappeared, she came out from the far end, circled the room, silently attacked him again from the rear, and again tore under the couch just in the nick of time.

Ginger, the intellectual dog, had been fooled by a mite of a kitten. Everybody had to laugh, even Ginger, who now showed he could take a joke. His tail began to wag. He began to enjoy himself. The kitten came out, and he and Pinky began to spar with each other, not in the bloody fashion with which he sparred with his enemy cats in Cranbury, but enjoying the bout in a good and sporting way.

When Pinky grew tired, she sat down on Ginger's front feet. "Aw-w-w," said Rachel. "We ought to have a picture of that."

Pinky cleaned her white paw. "It's her boxing mitt," said Jerry.

Rachel was overcome with love for Pinky. Much as she loved Ginger—after all she had helped to dust the pews that had earned the dollar that had bought Ginger in the first place—still, Ginger really counted as Jerry's dog because Jerry and Ginger were usually off somewhere together, the reservoir, East Rock, somewhere. And Gracie, the ancient New York cat, loved only Mama. No one else. Perhaps this kitten would love her, Rachel, the best.

That night, after supper, while they were all sitting on beach chairs outdoors, Pinky tried sparring with Gracie, but Gracie sent her spinning and then retired to the little roof over the small front porch that had already become her favorite spot in their new surroundings. From there, like an umpire, she could watch Ginger and Pinky spar, her head going back and forth dizzily and her tail waving like a signal.

"Oh, remind me," said Papa, as they all laughed at Gracie's bobbing head, "to close that little window up in the eaves when we go in."

But no one remembered to remind Papa because everyone was too engrossed with Pinky, the waif. "Come here, you sweet little bandit," said Rachel.

"Woe," said Pinky, and abandoning the game with Ginger, she sprang sideways toward Rachel, "*ss-ss-ss-ss,*" hissing and spitting as she came because she knew this was amusing.

"She knows me already," said Rachel.

4

The Typewriting Cat

For a while Pinky's chief pastime was sparring with Ginger. These sparring matches were spectacular, and it was hard for any member of the family to get any work done, for of course everyone had to watch. The minute Ginger and Pinky got out in the morning they started their sparring, which usually took place on the little boardwalk in front of the stoop.

Pinky would fall to right away. Pretending fury, she plastered back her ears, stood on her hind legs, and, giving the impression she was battling for her life, she socked at Ginger again and again. It was lucky that Ginger had had so much training with the cats of Cranbury or he might have made a poor showing. But he was very nimble and turned round and round, giving short happy yelps and hitting Pinky now and then lightly with his paw. Ginger was not a big dog and he was graceful, but compared to Pinky he seemed gigantic and clumsy.

The Pyes were not the only watchers. Pinky and Ginger usually had a large audience, and the larger it was, the better they sparred. Ladies on their way to the store had to stop and watch, and men on their way to the post office or to catch the boat stopped and watched too. Children often forgot to lick their ice-cream cones, and once in a while the wagon boys just didn't bother to meet boats at all but stayed to watch the match. So newcomers to the island called "Wagon! Wagon!" in vain.

Sitting on the stoop, watching Pinky and Ginger, Rachel felt her heart swell with pride and love. What a kitten she had! The show would end when all of a sudden Pinky would stop, just stop and walk off and clean her white paw, indicating she had wasted enough time now.

However, sparring was not Pinky's only accomplishment. She was a high jumper, and it was a beautiful sight to see her leap after a butterfly from the top of the stoop, in total abandon, not caring where she would land. It was as though she had the idea she could fly. And she loved to surprise people. She would appear from nowhere, race up a wispy, meager little bush, and as its topmost branch swayed under her fragile weight, she would intently survey the scene, pondering her next daring leap.

Rachel told people that Pinky was also learning to talk. Whenever Rachel walked past Pinky as the kitten lay sleeping on her becoming olive green pillow, Pinky always waked up enough to make a little remark. "Woe?" she inquired. "Oh-woe."

"It is short for 'Hello,'" explained Rachel, who could interpret everything that Pinky said.

Pinky had the entire family, including Papa, her first befriender, bewitched. Sometimes Gracie and Ginger, who up to this time had not been fond of one another, would stand side by side, heads lowered and dejected, mouths hanging open as they heard the words of endearment that used to fall only on them bestowed upon the enchanting kitten. They now had a common bond of jealousy. Once Ginger cried sadly when Jerry said something complimentary to Pinky. Jerry could not stand this and vowed never again to say anything nice to Pinky in the presence of his best friend, Ginger. "You're the best," he constantly had to reassure his sad-eyed dog.

To top all, Pinky was permitted to sit on Papa's lap as he typed his learned notes, his conclusions based on a day with the terns and quail!

In the beginning Pinky sat quietly enough, her little head going back and forth, intelligently following the sentences as they appeared on the blank paper. Next she tried catching the keys as they flew up. Naturally this smart game intrigued Papa, and he paused to see what she would do after that. She then tapped a key with one little front paw and, as it flew up, she caught it with the other front paw. Sometimes letters appeared palely on the paper. At first these pale letters coming on the hitherto white paper astonished Pinky; but then she performed this typing in a deliberate manner as though she knew what she was doing and what she was typing. From time to time she surveyed her results critically.

None of the Pyes had ever heard of such brightness in a cat, and they were overcome with admiration. Once Pinky actually spelled "woogie." This seemed to be a word, though no one had ever heard of it.

"It's probably in the big dictionary that we didn't bring," said Rachel. "That great big one that has everything in it."

"I wonder what woogie means," said Uncle Bennie.

No one, not even Rachel, could tell him. "But it's a word," she said. "There are plenty of words we don't know the meaning of."

"Oh, it's a word all right," said Uncle Bennie, and he ran off to circulate the news among his small beach friends. "We have a cat," he said to them, "that can typewrite." She had already typewritten the word of "woogie" he said, and other words that he did not know because he did not know how to read very well yet—it wasn't his birthday for some days.

So these little beach boys and girls came early the next day to see the typewriting cat typewrite. Twins named Janet and Joanne, who were Touhy Tomlinson's little sisters and Uncle Bennie's best friends on the beach, came first. "Where's the typewriting cat?" they asked. Having an older brother who teased them, they were skeptical and on guard not to be taken in by some fake. "Where's that cat that typed 'woogie'?" they demanded.

"Why," said Papa. "Here are Tweedledum and Tweedledee. Which is which, I wonder?"

The twins, already dressed for the beach in pink-and-white candy-striped bathing suits, smiled tolerantly and said again, "Where's that cat that typewrites?"

"She's having her milk," said Rachel.

The twins studied the kitten lapping up her milk, looking like a regular cat and not like a typewriting one. Their faces were expressionless, neither believing nor disbelieving.

"And we all have to have breakfast before we do anything else," said Mama.

"That's all right," said Janet, with Joanne saying the same thing a split second behind her. "We can watch." Over their bathing suits they had on thin little cotton jackets, though the morning air was quite crisp.

Their mother must be exactly the opposite of ours, thought Rachel. *She must think it's always warm instead of always cold, like ours.* "You know, twinsies," she said out loud, "we are going in swimming tomorrow too."

The twins said, "Of course. Why not?"

Uncle Bennie said to them, "Twins, do you know what day tomorrow is?"

"We forgotten," said they.

"Tomorrow is two things," said Uncle Bennie. "My birthday and I am four like you are. You *are* four, aren't you?"

"Maybe. Maybe not," said they.

"And it is the Fourth of July," Uncle Bennie went on. "The day when I have the revolution to stop sucking my thumb."

"We used to suck our thumbs, but Osie put something awful on them and so we stopped," said Janet.

"Who's Osie?" asked Uncle Bennie.

"Osie," they said.

"Oh," said Uncle Bennie.

Papa had a habit of drinking his coffee in a certain special way. The minute he picked up his cup with his right hand, he put the palm of his left hand under the cup and kept it there as he drank. Then his left hand escorted the cup from underneath back to its saucer again. Pinky leaped on Papa's lap to watch this process. The twins watched intently too, their eyes and heads, like Pinky's, traveling back and forth.

After a while Janet, the asker, asked, "Why do you hold your hand under your cup like that?"

"Yes, why?" asked Joanne, the emphasizer.

"To catch the drips," said Papa, "in case coffee has been spilled into my saucer. I don't want drops dripping on my tie or my shirt, do I? In the old days, coffee was always being spilled in my saucer, and there were drips on the bottom of my cup all the time. Of course, now that I am married to Mrs. Pye, there are never any drips on the bottom of my cup anymore. But my hand has this habit," said Papa, "and old habits are hard to break."

This was certainly a long speech for the twins to have to listen to when all they wanted was to see if it was really true that a typewriting cat lived here. They shifted their weight from one bare white foot to the other.

"Well," said Janet with a sigh. "Just say to yourself, 'I'm not going to do it.' And don't. It looks silly."

"You could make a Fourth-of-July revolution too," said Uncle Bennie. "Give it up the end of tomorrow at midnight, like I am my thumb."

"You are right," said Papa amiably. And he put his dry-bottomed cup, empty now, down on the dry saucer, folded his napkin neatly, pushed back his chair, and went to the typewriter, which was on a narrow little table in front of the window that looked out over the ocean. Janet and Joanne, like little automatons, followed. Uncle Bennie, Rachel, and Jerry followed them, tensely hoping their kitten would perform.

"Now you'll see," said Uncle Bennie to the twins.

"Maybe. Maybe not," they said.

Papa sat down. Pinky was in the middle of the floor, thinking.

"Let's get her," said Janet eagerly. "Let's get her and make her type."

"Oh, no," said Rachel. "We mustn't get her. She must come herself. She types because she wants to. No one makes her."

Papa typed a few words. Of course the sound of typing had become music to Pinky's ears, but it was her custom to give an impression of indifference. As the beguiling music continued, she skirted the room and loped toward Papa until she arrived at his feet as if by accident. She then cleaned her white paw and also her left ear, which she neatly turned inside out for the occasion. Then, shaking her head, she leaped onto Papa's lap, stood on her hind legs, sniffed the typewriter, and looked with interest at what Papa had written on the paper. She then sat down on Papa's lap.

"Will she do it now?" asked Janet breathlessly. "Will she typewrite now?" she asked, while Joanne's mouth parted speechlessly. Neither could bear the suspense. "Could she type 'woogie' again, do you think?" asked Janet.

Papa typed a few more words. As though she were pondering the words, Pinky watched alertly. Her eyes did not blink and she was quite unhurried as now, tentatively, she grabbed a key as it flew up. Then Papa let his hands fall to his sides and Pinky stood up, lightly resting one paw on the little table. She studied the keys.

"Studying," said Uncle Bennie delightedly. "It's not easy to typewrite, you know," he said accusingly to the twins.

"We know," they said. "You don't have to tell us."

Slowly, with one paw, her white one, Pinky began to tap the keys, and as a key hopped up, she grabbed it with her other front paw, the black one. Her little head was practically inside the typewriter as she played this fascinating game. It was cute and it was smart, but it was not typewriting. The twins watched impassively.

"Oh, spell something, spell something," groaned Uncle Bennie. What if she would not typewrite now? "Type," he urged. "Type."

And then, as though in answer to his prayers, Pinky sat back on her haunches and began to poke one key with one paw and another key with the other paw. It looked as though she were typing, and she was. These mysterious words appeared on the paper:

dop/go

The peppermint-striped twins scrutinized this achievement, but they said nothing. There might still be a catch to it, and they decided to remain unmoved. But the exuberance of Uncle Bennie and his exultant cry, "She can type, she can type! I told you she could type," and the respectful silence of the rest of the Pyes convinced the twins that these were words.

"What does that typing say?" asked Janet primly and not too eagerly, for it is not wise to act as though one has never before seen words typed by a typewriting cat. "Yes, what does it say?" echoed her sister, who was just as worldly wise. Janet and Joanne could not read yet, not even, "Let us run. Let us jump." But they knew real regular words when they saw them, and they suspected that words had been written.

"It says 'dop go,'" said Papa gravely.

"Dop go!" mused Janet. "Dop go!" she said, her little voice growing incredulous and pitched a little higher. "Joanne," she said. "It says, 'dop go.'"

"I know it," said Joanne. "You don't always have to tell me. It says 'dop go.' It means, Stop go."

With this the twins turned around, marched out of the cottage, and passed the word wherever they went that there was a kitten at Uncle Bennie's that could typewrite. First she typewrote "woogie." And just now she had typewritten "dop go." "Yes," they said proudly. "We saw her. Her name is Pinky."

Children rushed to the Pyes' to see the typewriting cat typewrite. That was all for today, however. Pinky yawned, jumped down, and stretched, first on her front paws and then on her back paws;

and then she ran to the side door to go out. So this time the thrill seekers had to content themselves with a sparring match, which was a good sight too, though not on a par with typewriting.

Papa had never been so carried away by a pet. You'd think that Papa, like that other bird man, Bish, who was on his way to the Washington zoo with his pet, his pygmy owl, would have chosen a bird pet, a canary at the least, and not a cat pet. But he hadn't. He was growing just as crazy about Pinky as Rachel was.

"Why not write a book about Pinky this summer, instead of the terns?" suggested Rachel as Papa pulled out the sheet with "dop/go" on it and put his tern sheet in. "Pinky's book," she said.

Papa looked at Rachel straight through his little square eyeglasses; and he didn't say anything.

5

The Grasshopper Hunt

Uncle Bennie's pet, the dead locust that he had brought from Cranbury, had worn out, and it was time to find a new pet. From dead locusts he had become interested in live ones—live locusts, live crickets, and live grasshoppers. "Do you think it is as easy to find grasshoppers here on this island," he asked his old dead pet, of which there was nothing left but the body, dry and brittle as an old bean pod, "as it used to be in that other town of Cranbury where there is grass, much more grass than here?" There being no answer from his pet, Uncle Bennie had to answer himself. "No," he said.

A plan was beginning to grow in Uncle Bennie's head. This plan was for him to capture enough crickets and grasshoppers to have a chorus in the house to sing to him in the nighttime. Is there anything nicer than to listen to crickets in the nighttime?

In the nighttime, safe from the cats and dog, they could sleep in the little secret room up in the eaves.

This room had little swinging doors to it, and Uncle Bennie could easily push these open. Then he could get inside and sleep with his crickets. But Mama forbade him to climb up there. He might break a leg, she said. Rachel would have to climb up and put his crickets in there every night. And he would have to listen, like the others, from below.

In the daytime he could carry a cricket around with him in his pocket. It might sing as he walked along the path. People might say, "Where's that cricket?" When he wanted a certain particular cricket to take for a walk, Rachel would get it for him. "The one in the red box," he'd say. Or, "The blue one."

Rachel was not fond of crickets and grasshoppers in the sunny fields. The way they would hop at her and get in her hair! But she probably would not object to just one grasshopper at a time in a box, or one cricket, for she was very fond of Uncle Bennie and minded him like a true uncle. Sometimes she pretended that he was an old uncle instead of a little one and would hand him a cane to hobble with.

So after luncheon Uncle Bennie sauntered out of the cottage and went around to the side where the long grass grew. He sat down to await a cricket or some live bug. My! What luck so soon! There was a sandy-colored grasshopper sitting as still as though it were a part of the reed it was on. The grasshoppers here were not as green as those in Cranbury. That was natural, since the grass here was not as green either.

"Come, grasshopper," Uncle Bennie begged, moving an inch. But it is one thing to see a grasshopper and another to catch it. And this one hopped so fast that Bennie had no idea where it had hopped to. Just one big hop and it was gone. That was all.

Uncle Bennie lay down on his stomach and peered through the faded grass, hoping for a return of the grasshopper. That grasshopper didn't come back but a neat little cricket came along. It looked at Uncle Bennie sideways, out of one eye. Uncle Bennie eyed it back. He cupped his hands and waited patiently. He lay very still hoping the cricket would jump into his hands. The cricket didn't jump into them but a ladybug did. Something was the matter with one of her wings. It was out of order, so she couldn't fly very well. Well, she could be bait for the cricket. Uncle Bennie had not asked for any bait, but bait had come to him.

From the windowsill, inside the house, Pinky had observed Uncle Bennie with great interest as he tried to catch the sandy-colored grasshopper. She had seen its farewell leap, and she knew how disappointed Uncle Bennie must be. Seeing that the noisy fellow, as she had named Uncle Bennie, was after more prey, she decided to enter the game. She had not had one single cricket or grasshopper to eat since she had entered this house of refinement, just milk, oatmeal, and food that was terribly tasteless after the baby crabs and minnows she was used to. She thought to herself, *It's no wonder the noisy fellow gets tired of never having a cricket or a grasshopper to eat. I do too.*

Pinky was quite adjusted to life in this house now, and, aside from the tasteless fare, she liked it. However, she was not used to being waited on hand and foot, and when she made a decision, as now, to go out, she was not going to ask someone to let her out. She had often observed how the food giver, as she had named Mama, unfastened the hook on the screen to shoo out flies and then fastened it again. Pinky knew she could get out that way, and who cared about getting in? Not she.

So now she worked and worked on the little hook until at last she unlatched it and could push the screen open. The screen swung up, and with it resting lightly on her thin bony back she balanced on the sill for a moment and then leaped silently to the ground. The screen swung down and closed behind her, giving only the slightest sort of squeak.

Daintily and quietly Pinky sidled along in a roundabout route to mislead any watcher as to her true destination. Finally she landed right next to

Uncle Bennie, who was so absorbed he had no idea he now had company in the hunt. His companion took up her position nearby in a small clump of wispy grass, and she, too, waited. She watched the ladybug crawling over Uncle Bennie's hands, for nothing was too small or trivial for her complete and earnest study.

Then, aware that Uncle Bennie's eyes were fixed unblinkingly on something, she looked where they were looking and saw the cricket. The cricket was eyeing the ladybug. The ladybug in lovely innocence was only trying to put her wing in order. Uncle Bennie was eyeing the cricket and now Pinky was eyeing the cricket likewise. Pinky's stomach was full and she was in no great hurry for food. Right now education was what Pinky was interested in. How a boy caught a cricket. She watched, now the cricket, now the ladybug, and now Uncle Bennie, approvingly.

Uncle Bennie decided that just lying on his stomach with a ladybug tickling his hand would not catch the cricket. He began wiggling, squirming, lying still, feigning sleep, yet, inch by inch, making a little headway toward the cricket. When he was quite close, he leaned on his elbow, held out the hand that had the ladybug in it toward the cricket, and hoped the cricket would be tempted to hop into this hand.

At last the cricket did jump. Pinky's tail gave a twitch and her eyes followed the cricket, but otherwise not a muscle moved. The cricket had not jumped into the palm of the noisy fellow but over his head somewhere. Both Uncle Bennie and Pinky slowly revolved. Hurray! There was the cricket. He had hopped right behind Uncle Bennie and was brightly eyeing him again.

He likes me, thought Uncle Bennie. *He wants to be my pet.* "Come here," he coaxed.

Until now Pinky had not had a very great respect for Uncle Bennie. He was so noisy! But now he was being as quiet as she was, and she found herself admiring him. He was pondering his moves carefully, he was in no hurry, he was persistent, and she had a feeling he would win. His pleasing, rather husky voice apparently made a favorable impression on the cricket, for all of a sudden it hopped right into the palm of Uncle Bennie's hand. This happened just in the nick of time, for Pinky, deciding not to let admiration lead her out of the bounds of reason and drooling for too long over a postponed treat, had leaped for the cricket at the very same moment that it had hopped. But she missed it because, like a tiddlywink, it had already popped into the cup of Uncle Bennie's hands, which were gently closing together, and Uncle Bennie had caught his first alive Fire Island pet, a cricket, rather small and with a pretty voice. It gave an inquiring little chirp as though to say, "Oh, where am I?"

"Don't worry," said Uncle Bennie softly. "You are going to be my best pet. I won't let the cats get you—go away, Pinky!—and all you need to do is to eat and drink and sing."

Pinky was smugly cleaning her white paw. She was pretending that she had meant for her pounce to send the cricket into Uncle Bennie's hands and that otherwise she had no interest in the cricket. Then, paw suspended in midair, she cocked her head and studied the uncle. He really had done well. Was he going to eat the cricket? No. Not now. He put it in his pocket, a rather torn airy pocket in his short pants. Well, quite often she, too, did not eat what she had caught the minute she caught it. Tuck a battered mouse under something, pretend to go away—mouse would come to life, attempt to escape—pounce on it again, play with it some more, and then, eat it up! That was a very good game.

Uncle Bennie was talking to his captive. "I'm naming you Sam, after Sam Doody, the Boy Scout boy."

Uncle Bennie happily wandered off with Pinky following furtively. He searched in all the clumps of grass around the cottage looking for another pet. He fell into what he hoped was not poison ivy. In case it was, he rubbed his hands off good on his legs, so he was sure he had rubbed the poison away. He just couldn't catch another cricket. But he didn't care. He had this one wonderful cricket.

"Hello in there, Sam," he said to the inhabitant of his pocket.

As Uncle Bennie returned to the cottage, Pinky bounded along behind him. Rachel caught Pinky up in her arms and spoke softly in the kitten's ear. "Where have you been?"

Pinky purred. All day yesterday and so far this morning whenever Rachel came near her, Pinky purred. "She loves me," said Rachel.

"Well, don't let her get my cricket," said Uncle Bennie.

"Let's see it," said Rachel, looking in Uncle Bennie's pocket. The little brown cricket looked up at Rachel. "Oh, he's real cute," she said.

"He sings," said Uncle Bennie proudly.

Uncle Bennie carried the cricket around with him all day, and the cricket seemed to like it. Now and then he chirped. Uncle Bennie liked him.

During the afternoon Papa worked very hard putting up a huge green umbrella he had bought from the Army and Navy store. It was oblong in shape, more like a roof than an umbrella, and strong ropes on all four corners tied to staves in the ground held it securely down. Papa had put it up on the ocean side of The Eyrie, and it was spacious enough for all the family and even some guests to sit under on a hot day and look out over the wide Atlantic. While Papa was finishing up, Uncle Bennie sat nearby on the sand and spoke occasionally to his cricket.

Papa was very interested in the cricket. *He likes my cricket because, even though it's not a bird, still it can fly,* thought Uncle Bennie.

"In China," said Papa, "the boys have cricket cages and exchange crickets with one another, trying to get the best singer or fighter."

"Mine is a good singer," said Uncle Bennie proudly. "I don't know about the fights."

"Where are you going to keep him at night?" asked Mama, who was standing by with hammer and screwdriver to help Papa with the big umbrella.

"Oh, I know where," said Uncle Bennie secretively.

"We don't want Gracie or Pinky to get him," said Mama. "Cats love crickets and grasshoppers, but they are bad for the cats. They make cats thin and scrawny, too many of them do."

"Well, the cats are worse for the grasshoppers," said Uncle Bennie. "To be eaten alive is worse than to be thin and scrawny."

Uncle Bennie told about the faded sandy-colored grasshopper that had escaped. "They are not as green here as in Cranbury," he said. "Do you remember how green they are there?"

Then Papa told about the greenest grasshopper he had ever seen in his life. It was out in California and, "I'm sorry to have to say it," said Papa, "but this very green grasshopper was the evening meal of that baby owl of Hiram Bish's I told you about; and that little owl ate up that green green grasshopper as though it were celery, with a cru-unch."

"Oh-h-h," groaned Uncle Bennie. "Well, he can't get my cricket. Because he's there and we're here."

In the evening, after supper, Uncle Bennie fixed up a little box for his cricket cage. He drew black bars on it so it would look like a real cage. He put some ants in it for the cricket to eat and a few drops of water in a tiny tin doll's plate for it to drink. "Pretend it's dew," he said to Rachel. He also put a little clump of grass in to make the cricket feel really at home. Then he whispered good night to his new pet and asked Rachel to put it up in the eaves for him, so Rachel put a chair on a table and climbed up. Then she shoved the cricket in his cage inside the little swinging doors.

It was cool in the eaves, but Rachel had not noticed that nor had she noticed that the little porthole window was still open because she had not stayed up there long enough even to look in.

So far no one had remembered to remind Papa to close that porthole window. Often Papa had said, "Remind me . . ." And then he would stop. Everyone would wait for him to go on with what they were supposed to remind him about. But he never went on. That was the way with Papa. He would start to say something and then he would stop, forgetting that he had everyone alerted for some remark or another, forks halfway to mouths, glasses suspended in midair. Papa was really very absentminded. If someone asked him a question, he might have to speak to Papa three times before Papa said, "What?"

"Are you listening?" the person would say and would not go on with the conversation until Papa would answer gently and as though from far away,

"Yes?" The person would then speak quickly before Papa went inside himself again, far, far away. "With his birds," explained Rachel.

So the porthole window was still open. But the weather was nice, so it really didn't matter whether it was open or not.

Now Uncle Bennie got into bed. He sucked his thumb. This was the last night for that. The cricket gave one or two plaintive chirps. "Did you hear those?" he asked Rachel.

"Mm-m-m," she said.

"Sleep tight," Uncle Bennie called to his cricket. "Sing. And then, sleep tight."

6

Pinky's Narrow Escape

Today was the Fourth of July. It had been an important day for that reason and for many other reasons. For instance, the kitten had typed "grog." ("I think she meant to say 'frog' but 'grog' is pretty good, isn't it?" said Rachel.) And the family had had their first swim of the year. In the morning it had been a little cloudy. "Oh, don't rain, don't rain," begged the children. They had been here forever and had not gone in swimming yet!

But the clouds had blown over and the children had had their first swim. The surf boomed and roared, and Rachel and Jerry soon learned to ride in on the waves and to dive through them. Swimming was impossible, but Jerry and Rachel called jumping in the surf swimming, and Uncle Bennie said to the biggest waves, "Watch out for Uncle Bennie," and tore way back to the dune in delighted terror when they came pounding in.

"We'll come every day in the afternoon," Mama promised them. "That is, every day that is nice," she added, and took one last dive herself through a mountainous wave.

What a wonderful mama! thought Rachel when Mama staggered out on the beach, blinded, laughing, dripping. People called her mother frail because she wore a size-two shoe. *She might look frail but she isn't frail,* said Rachel to herself. Mama had a lovely voice and tra-la-la, you could hear her singing as she went about her work. *Does that sound frail?* She even stroked Papa's head in the evening when the dishes were washed and Papa had had a hard day of thinking.

And of course, besides the first swim, today had been Uncle Bennie's birthday. "Happy birthday to you, happy birthday to you," had been sung, the four candles blown, the wish made, and the cake eaten. So the day had been important and the night was going to be important too. Uncle Bennie was going to stop sucking his thumb on the stroke of midnight.

Now supper was over. The dishes were washed and the sun had set. It was growing dark, and one of the best things about this particular Fourth of July was soon to begin. That is, the fireworks across the bay. The Pyes were not going to cross the bay to watch; they were going to stroll down to the dock, sit on the edge, dangle their legs above the water, sip sodas, and watch.

Since it was eight o'clock, Papa suggested they get started for the bay now, buy their cones or sodas, whatever the plan was, and prepare to view the pyrotechnics, a long word meaning fireworks.

Papa liked words beginning with "py." Naturally, why not, with the name Pye to begin with? This may have been one reason why Papa was so fond of their new pet, Pinky. And it is a wonder he did not suggest spelling her name Pynky instead, for it is possible to use a "y" instead of an "i." But neither he nor anyone else had thought of doing that. Anyway, her name began with "P" and ended with "y." That's almost Pye. And think of the pygmy owl, that bird of the Bishes' out West that Papa had made the acquaintance of recently. You would think that pygmy owls would be Papa's favorite birds since they began with "py," and maybe they were, though Papa always said he loved all birds and no one kind in particular. The pygmy owl happened to be the favorite bird of that other ornithologist, Mr. Hiram Bish, whose name began with "Bi" and not "py."

These were the thoughts of Rachel as the Pyes strolled across the island. And she thought it was too bad that pineapple and pine are not spelled with "py" instead of "pi" because pineapple was Papa's favorite fruit and he loved the smell of pine—outdoors, not in the house, for he hated pine soap.

Pinky and Ginger accompanied the Pyes and were going to view the pyrotechnics too, but Gracie had to stay behind. She was such a well-adjusted cat she did not mind. The children stopped at the drugstore and bought pink soda and some ice-cream cones, and then they went out onto the wharf where the boats docked. Other people were there too, to watch the fireworks and to wait for the last boat. Which would be first, the Pyes wondered, the pyrotechnics or the boat? They sat down on the silver gray seawall and listened to the water below them lapping against the dark piles, and they waited for the daylight to wane entirely from the sky, for then the fireworks would begin.

On Fire Island itself there were to be no fireworks. But a few of the wagon boys began lighting sparklers they had probably brought from the mainland because nothing for the Fourth, not even punk, was sold here. Touhy Tomlinson gave Jerry one. There were more and more things about Fire Island that Mama liked. No fireworks was the best so far. She wished The Eyrie could be theirs, and then the family could come here every summer. Mrs. Pulie didn't want The Eyrie anymore. She was building a big and elegant cottage and had even planted great green plants called "elephant's ears," an unusual plant for Fire Island, in front of it.

Ginger went sniffing all over the wharf rapidly, and as though he were on the trail of something very important. Snort! He blew the sand out of his nose from time to time and sometimes he gave a firm sneeze. What delight when he found the tip end of an old ice-cream cone! Pinky was peeking at herself over the edge of the wharf.

"Be careful, Pinky," said Rachel. "You'll fall in." She picked Pinky up and held her in her lap.

It was a beautiful evening. There was a thin slice of moon in the west, and in a line below it were

several planets. "A striking display especially for the Fourth!" observed Mama.

Then they spotted the lighted boat coming. Laughter echoed across the waves. It was not the little boat, the *Maid of the Bay*, which had brought the Pyes when they came, but the big one with several decks that was used when large crowds were expected and much luggage.

As the boat floated in, a gentle breeze brought a whiff of a fragrant cigar. A man's voice called out from above, "Hello, darling." "Hello, dear," answered a lady's loving voice, clear and bell-like.

The only thing missing, thought Rachel blissfully, *is the smell of punk. If we had punk, we would have everything*. As if she had read her thoughts, her mother handed her a long thin packet of crinkling bright red paper. It had smudged gold letters on it, Chinese letters, and it could hold only one thing, slender sticks of Chinese punk.

"Now," said Papa, lighting a stick for each. "We are ready for the pyrotechnics." He put his piece of punk between his toes. Papa, their dignified Papa, was barefoot!

"Edgar!" Mama had said. "You can't go barefoot to the wharf! "

"Why not?" said Papa. "I have a blister on my heel."

It seemed to Rachel that Papa was very carefree

down here on this island, and she put her punk between her toes, too, to be exactly like him.

Now the fireworks began. The first ones went up with a sudden splash of color directly across the bay—shimmering showers of blue and gold and purple and red, lovely and liquid in the velvety darkness. Soon, all the way up and down the Long Island shore, from as far away as they could see, there were clusters of fiery color.

"Those must be from Babylon," said Papa.

"Babylon!" exclaimed Uncle Bennie. "Zowie!" It sounded far and Biblical.

Then the show was over. First one little town and then another sank back into anonymous darkness. Only an occasional lone Roman candle or a skyrocket could be seen. Still, it was so pleasant sitting here watching the moving lights of a fishing boat home late, or of a pleasure launch, speculating as to which town certain far lights belonged, and hearing the waves gulping below, that none of the Pyes wanted to go home. Everyone else had left, but the Pyes could not tear themselves away. They felt as though they were afloat on a large and tranquil craft.

Then the peepers began their wild and lonesome singing, shrill and growing louder as they all took it up.

And then a group of rowdies came noisily out on the wharf, guffawing loudly, shattering the serenity of the night. And suddenly Rachel cried, "Pinky! Pinky! Where's Pinky?" She had been so engrossed with the sights and sounds of the evening she had lost track of Pinky. She couldn't even remember Pinky getting off her lap. "Where is she?" moaned Rachel.

Everybody leaped up. The noise of the rowdies became louder as they came farther out on the wharf. They were all pretending they were marching, and the one who was leading this march was holding something straight out in front of him, stiffly and roughly. As he came near, a dim light from the recently moored big boat showed the Pyes what he was carrying, and one little white paw gleaming in the darkness told them for certain that this roughneck had their Pinky!

He was headed right for the edge of the wharf. What was he going to do? Drop Pinky in the sea?

"Hold on! Wait!" shouted all the Pyes, emerging from the blackness.

"What're you doing with our cat?" demanded Papa.

"Don't bodder dat cat!" yelled Uncle Bennie, jumping up and down.

Rachel screamed with horror and Jerry rolled up his sleeves. Ginger barked at all of them, wondering if it would be all right to bite. The rowdies were taken by surprise, and the one holding Pinky sheepishly handed her to Papa. Then the marchers turned and, laughing raucously again, they disappeared.

"Were they really going to drop Pinky in the water?" asked Rachel.

"She would have drowned. It's deep here," said Jerry.

"The wicked hooligans!" said Mama.

They were so relieved that Pinky was safe and sound they crowded around her, comforting her.

"Woe," said Pinky, the heroine, plaintively. "Woe."

Then Papa, who had a slow-rising anger—it was just as hard for him as for the children to think anyone could be so wicked as to drown a cat—suddenly became terribly angry. "Where'd they go?" he demanded. "Where'd they go? I'd like to punch them in the nose," he said, and he stalked, barefooted though he was and with a piece of burnt punk still between his two middle toes, after the rowdies.

All the others followed. "Edgar, dear," said Mama beseechingly. "Be careful," she said. "That sort of hooligan is capable of anything."

But the hooligans had disappeared in the darkness, leaving behind an echo of their noise and raucousness, continuing with their carousing and bent on more mischief, no doubt.

"I should have punched them on the nose right then and there," said Papa, striding on ahead.

It is doubtful if Papa, who was a gentle person, had ever punched anyone on the nose or chin in his life. He was not at all like people in moving pictures who are always punching somebody else. But now Papa's pale hair was bristling and so was his sandy beard, and he really looked as though he would have punched those men on the chin. In fact, he looked as though that was what he did most of the time, punch people on chins.

Everyone held his breath and was quiet out of respect to this new and unusual Papa. They were glad when he recovered his composure, gave up the pursuit, and rejoined them. "They have been imbibing too freely," he said.

"You mean yo ho ho and a bottle of rum? Pirates?" asked Uncle Bennie, coming closer to Mama's skirts.

"They were wicked robbers, weren't they, Mama?" said Rachel. "Oh, dear! Last year someone stole Ginger. Suppose this year someone should steal Pinky?"

"No," said Mama. "They won't bother her anymore. They don't want her. They just happened to see her and thought what fun it would be to drop a kitten in the water. Smart alecks!"

"Listen to her heart," crooned Rachel, her ear close to Pinky. "How it's pounding!"

Papa became angry all over again. "I should have punched them. I'm going after them. They should be locked up," he said, turning around suddenly. In doing so, a very unfortunate thing happened to Papa. His foot slipped off the edge of the boardwalk, and he twisted his ankle. He had to hobble home and, though he didn't say, "Ouch," everyone knew his ankle hurt or he would be walking on it. It was swelling up so much Mama put hot and cold compresses on it, hoping one or the other would work.

Feeling subdued, everyone got ready for bed right away. Uncle Bennie wondered if, in view of the accident, he might *not* give up sucking his thumb tonight, give it up tomorrow night instead when no robbers would be around and Papa's foot would be all right. Still, it was his birthday now, right now, and he was four years old.

"I'll pray," he said to himself. "Dear God, help me to stop sucking my thumb, now I'm four. I just can't help doing it." "I'll help you," he answered for God. And then he said for himself, "I'll give it up on the five of July if I can't make it tonight. Thank you for the help," he said to God. "And the answer."

Well, it was not midnight yet. He began to suck his thumb. "Wake me up at midnight, will you, Rachel?" he said.

But there was no answer, for Rachel was asleep with Pinky, no worse for her adventure, sleeping above Rachel's head on her pillow. In the eaves, however, Uncle Bennie's cricket gave a chirp.

"Says he will," thought Uncle Bennie, glad to have the problem solved.

7

Pinky Meditates

In the morning Papa's foot still hurt him, and as it was very swollen, it was decided he'd better go over to Bay Shore and have it X-rayed.

"Does it hurt to have a foot exerated?" asked Rachel anxiously.

"Oh, no," said Mama. "We just want to make sure no bones are broken."

Of course all the children wanted to go with him. "We've been on this island forever," pleaded Rachel.

"We've been on a boat only once, the day we came," said Bennie.

"Phew! What a life!" said Mama.

But in the end the entire family went, with the exception of Mama, who said she would stay home with the cricket and the other pets.

They had to race for the boat, for it had already blown its first whistle. It was the big boat that they had seen come in last night, not the little *Maid of the Bay,* and they had never been on it. "We could go to Europe in this," said Jerry.

"Please bring me some lentils, if you can, if you see a store," Mama yelled up to them as they stood waving to her from the sunny deck. "Would you believe it," she explained to the lady standing next to her, "they don't even have any lentils in the store here?"

So the family went and the foot got X-rayed and the family came back.

"Well," said Mama, who had gone to the boat with Ginger to meet them. "How is it?"

Papa had his foot in a cast! And he was walking with a crutch the doctor had loaned him. "It's a fracture," he said. "I have to stay off it for a while."

Oh, dear, thought Rachel. What now of his work on the terns and on all the other birds that he was here to observe for those men in Washington? Aloud she said, "I'll watch the birds for you, Papa. I'll try to find out something for you and you can send it in. The other day I thought I saw a cormorant."

"You'll be a real help," said Papa. "I know you will."

Papa was not a complaining man, and since he had a great deal of work in his briefcase to catch up on, he could certainly keep busy. That is, he could keep busy if Pinky would let him do a little typing for a change, instead of her. This backlog of work that he had could occupy him for a long time, work, for instance, on the genus Eupsychortyx, a group of quail about which he had pages and pages of notes and sketches.

But would this satisfy the men in Washington? Would they be content with a study of quail in Santa Marta when what they were counting on was a study of the birds of Fire Island? That was what had to be found out, and Papa eased himself into his chair under the big green umbrella and, with injured foot resting on a stool and with a small table that fitted nicely over his lap for his typewriter, he composed a letter presenting his predicament to the men in Washington.

What he wanted to know was this. Did they wish to withdraw him from this job and send another ornithologist out here? He did not know how long he was going to be laid up. But he did know that he would be quite limited for a while in his activity, at least his foot activity, he wrote, though so far his brain activity could be counted on to remain as usual. After this letter was finished, he put a piece of blank paper in the typewriter. He was accustomed to work, and just because he had a lame foot, he was not going to bask under the green umbrella and do nothing.

Pinky, on the back stoop, had heard Papa typewriting his letter. The reason she had not come over to help him was that she had been practicing leaps, taking off from the stoop exaltedly after a yellow butterfly. Having had the breath knocked out of her from one completely abandoned flight, she had had to rest a moment. Then, peeking at Papa from time to time out of the corner of her eye and washing herself meanwhile, she finally decided to lope over to him. She sprang up on his lap and waited patiently for him to begin to typewrite. However, Papa's long nimble fingers did not begin at once, for Papa was somehow confused as to just what work to go on with until he had had an answer from the men in Washington. Sometimes it is hard to switch one's mind from Fire Island birds to birds of Santa Marta, and so, closing his eyes, Papa sat back. Taking in the situation at a glance, Pinky saw that she would have to play the typewriter herself. She started clicking the letters very slowly. *Pul-ink, pul-unk.*

In the cottage everyone was happy to hear the sound of the typewriter, for it meant that, since Papa was at work, he was happy. So Mama suggested that, since Papa was happy, she and the children might as well go down to the beach for a cooling dip in the ocean.

Jerry and Bennie jumped at the idea. This morning Jerry had brought home the bottom of a baby carriage that still had all its original four wheels on their axles. The wheels were not even very bent.

"Where'd you get those wheels?" Uncle Bennie had asked when Jerry had appeared from behind a fisherman's shack on the dock with his treasure.

"Back there," said Jerry. "The man back there just said, 'Take it, son, take it. Glad to get rid of it. Junk,' he said. 'Just junk.'"

"Junk!" Uncle Bennie had exclaimed. "The way

people, big people, get things mixed up!" he'd thought. "The best things in the world are junk to most people."

Now Jerry and Uncle Bennie hoped to find boards drifting in on the beach that they could put on top of these excellent wheels, and then Jerry would practically have his wagon taxi completed. So naturally Jerry and Uncle Bennie were anxious to go down there. "Hurry up, Rachel," said Jerry impatiently. "Get your suit on."

But Rachel wondered if she should go down to the beach. She thought she should not abandon Papa on the first day of his fractured ankle. Then she thought, yes, she should go down to the beach and study the birds for him. Some Pye ought to be studying birds, so she put on her bathing suit after all. Papa was typing—she could hear him—or Pinky was typing. Anyway some typing was going on, so Papa would not need her. She ran to kiss him good-bye, and glancing at his paper, which did not have very much on it (*Hasn't warmed up yet,* Rachel thought), she was rather surprised to have the word "cat" pop out at her quite often from the paper. Then she reasoned, "Must be writing about the genius catbird," and she raced off to catch up with the family. "Back soon," she called to her father.

Pul-ink. Pul-unk. Beginning slowly but soon gathering speed, the typewriter sounded like the cackling certain blackbirds make early in the morning. What appeared on the paper was this:

Meditations of Pinky Pye

My name is Pinky because that is my name. I was named it.

"Woogie" was the first word that I typewrote. What does it mean? It means what it sounds like—woogie. It is not yet in the dictionary. When it does get in the dictionary, it will come between woofy and woohoo.

Usually the first word people type is their name. Going by this, Woogie should be my name. But it isn't because Pinky is my name.

"Pinky! Why not Blackie?" ask those two little ones who in their pink stripes are alike.

I have to stick out my raspberry-colored tongue to show them.

"Oh, yes, of course," they say. "It is like pink ice cream."

True. Only my tongue is hot, not cold.

To me, genealogies are tiresome. The genealogy of the old cat, Gracie, for instance, is a boring one recited to all visitors. Gracie is, they say, the daughter of a famous New York cat named Ash-can Sam. Since so much is made of genealogies around here, I feel obliged to put in a few words about my past.

I am the daughter of a brave mother who was abandoned last summer by horrible summer people. The less said about my father the better. In winding up my genealogy, I will say that my mother, too, claimed to be the daughter of a famous New York cat named Ash-can Sam. I believe that all cats from New York are daughters of this infamous cat called Ash-can Sam. So, why people make such a big thing of Gracie being *the* New York cat, I don't know. My mother was a cat of some repute, too, but I never heard her boast about it. Her Ash-can

Sam father was coal black, a handy color. My brother and sisters are white with orange and black and tan spots, excellent for camouflage, but they are not beautiful as I am. Still they know how to catch crabs without getting pinched. Do you?

Soon after I and my brother and sisters were born, my brave mother caught cold and died. We mewed for two days (our eyes were barely open) and then we had to make our living as we could. Using our wits, we caught minnows, baby frogs, and insects. And we stayed alive. I love to reminisce about my babyhood in the reeds and rushes, for it was a happy life full of danger.

Then, one day, mistaking us for crabs I suppose, an awful girl captured us in a crab net and that was the end of that life for us. Where my brother and sisters are, I don't know. But I am here with Pye.

Now Pye is, they say, a famous bird man, though I have never seen him catch a bird and eat one. My mother was more famous, for she caught them. Pye contents himself with just watching the birds, a pastime we all enjoy. In this place watching is a very important thing. Even the cook, who is known as "Mama," is aware of this. "Watch out for poison ivy." "Watch out you don't drown." Or just plain, "Wat-chout!" Everyone in this house likes to watch something or other. The noisy fellow, Bennie, watches crickets. He catches them, at least, though he doesn't eat them any more than Pye does birds. So far, I haven't got the hang of why all this watching is going on and no catching. There must be some good reason, and the minute I have caught on I'll explain it to you, who must be as much in the fog as I am.

Well, here come the two-alike in their peppermint stripes, marching around the house, wanting to see me typewrite. It's too bad they missed the show, for I am through for the day. Still, why not practice a little, get up my speed?

As the twins marched up, "Urra, urra, urra, urra," were the words they saw on the paper.

"What does that say?" they asked deferentially.

"It says, 'urra, urra, urra, urra,'" said Papa courteously.

"What does that mean?"

"It either means 'Hurray!' or it means Pinky is purring on the typewriter."

Since there seemed no reason for Pinky to be saying "Hurray!" the twins decided that she was purring. They then hastened off to spread the latest news about Pinky, that this typewriting cat could now even purr on the typewriter, the hardest thing yet.

8

The Big Blow

A few days later Papa received a letter from the senator from Connecticut saying he was sorry about Papa's accident and imploring him, "Stay on, Mr. Pye, and do your work." The letter said that the same old rule prevailed in Washington of "calling in Pye," broken-footed or not, and no one would consider sending any other bird man to Fire Island in Papa's place. The senator ended up by saying, "I am sending you a wheelchair that I bought some years ago when I broke my leg in a trout stream. Perhaps you can get around in that."

"A wheelchair!" exclaimed Uncle Bennie in delight. "Can I ride in it?"

"Sure," said Papa. "Because I know I won't."

Nevertheless, today when the wheelchair arrived on the early morning boat, Papa had been very pleased with it. Though he had never been in one before in his life, he knew how to ride it right away. He was pretty tired of sitting under the green umbrella, seeing the same view all the time, even if it was a marvelous view. Of course he had been hobbling around on one foot with the help of a cane, but this was pretty tiring, and he had not been able to get down on the sandy beach for long walks at all. Now with the help of the wheelchair he could get on with the study of the Fire Island birds a little better, though he still couldn't do any hunting in difficult places for hidden nesting sites.

"Papa, won't you have to get permission to go around in a wheelchair?" asked Rachel. "After all a wheelchair is something on wheels, isn't it? And I thought only bikes and wagons were allowed in the wheel line."

So before Papa went careening around in his wheelchair and possibly getting arrested for being on wheels, he decided to find out the rules and regulations.

"It's all right with me," said the man in charge of such affairs. "That is, if you get a little bell," he said to Papa. "Ring it goin' around corners." The Pyes couldn't tell whether the man was joking or not, so they bought Papa a bell. Now Gracie and Pinky and Papa all had little bells. As a heavy fog had blown in, it was very handy to have the little bell, and on the return trip home Papa rang it whenever he thought someone was coming.

This was the first real foggy day the Pyes had

had since their arrival twelve days ago. Rachel and Uncle Bennie and Jerry decided to go for a walk in the fog. They couldn't get lost in a fog on this island. They knew the narrow walks by heart.

They walked along the top of the dune, and it was so foggy they couldn't see the ocean down below, though they could hear it pounding in. They felt eerie being this close to the mighty Atlantic Ocean, with nothing between them and Europe but the invisible ocean. They listened to it booming. It might be rising and rising in the fog, unseen, and soon it might swell up and over them. Suddenly feeling scared, they decided to go home without one single roll down the dune. Can you imagine rolling down a sand dune not knowing when you might meet ocean instead of real, right, regular beach? No. Neither could they. So they started for home.

What an unusual sort of day it was! First there was fog. And now it was beginning to grow windy. Gusts of wind blew fog away in patches, revealing here a cottage and there a tree and once the peppermint-striped twins playing house as though there wasn't any fog at all.

On the way home the children stopped to pick up the mail. They felt grown-up and smart because no one had said, "Please pick up the mail on the way home." They just knew to do it.

"Well, I'm four," said Uncle Bennie when they

reached home and were praised for this thoughtfulness.

"Br-r-r," said Mama when they came in. "I thought you'd never get back. I don't like you traipsing around in the fog and the cold. One thing I hate is a cold, wet summer at the beach."

"Oh, Mama. That's what you always say at the least sign of a cloud. It's not going to be a cold, wet summer at the beach. It's going to be a nice summer," said Rachel comfortingly. "It *is* a nice summer already."

Mama lighted the log fire in the fireplace.

"Besides," Rachel added. "You know it rains once in a while even in Cranbury. Anyway, it's not raining. It's fogging."

"It seems wetter when it rains or fogs at the beach than it does at home," said Mama, blowing on a log.

"Well. We don't have to put on our winter underwear," said Uncle Bennie. "It's not that cold, is it? We don't need that, do we? That means it's hot, not cold, if we don't need that." And he said, "Phew!" in disgust, and sat down in a little red rocker in front of the fire with his crickets in their cage on his lap. "Sing, Sams," he said. And one sang.

Uncle Bennie had three crickets now, and in the daytime he carried them around in a box that was like an apartment house, for he had put walls in to make rooms, a room apiece for each cricket. Why? Because (I'm sorry to have to say this, but it is true) many crickets cannot stand each other. They will begin to fight if they find another cricket trying to come into their house, and whoever wins will (I'm sorry to have to say this sad but true fact, too) eat up the one that he has beaten. Uncle Bennie had had this experience, and, in case you do not believe me, you may certainly believe him, for he *knew*. That is why he kept them separated.

Papa was going over the mail. "What do you know!" he said. "Here's a card from Hiram Bish, mailed in Havana. 'Sightseeing here for a few hours,' it says. 'Owl liking boat trip. We are too.' It's signed, 'Myra, Hi, and Owlie.'"

"Where do you suppose his boat is now?" asked Jerry.

"Well . . ." said Papa. "It takes about twelve days from California to New York. He must be coming in today or tomorrow."

"Unless he is lost in the fog," said Uncle Bennie forebodingly.

All day foghorns had been sounding, and now and then it seemed as though the deep, insistent blast of an ocean liner could be heard. Papa said this was possible. Liners going to and coming from Europe, though not, of course, those from South America or the West Coast, could be seen by the Pyes. And if they could be seen by them, then they could probably be heard by them, too, in a fog.

There was a sudden and swift and very strong gust of wind. Fog blew past the windows of The Eyrie like smoke. The fire flared up in the fireplace. The oil lamps sputtered and smoked. Papa rolled to the window in his wheelchair and looked out. (He was getting so fond of his wheelchair he rolled around the house whenever possible.)

"Fog's lifting," he said. "Quite a wind has sprung up, and it will blow the fog right out to sea. So, Mama, it will probably be sunny tomorrow and you won't have your cold, wet summer at the beach."

Mama smiled. She didn't care when people teased her. "If that's the case," she said, "we better have at least one nice hot supper in front of the open fire." And this they did.

By the time supper was over the wind had reached a tremendous force. Papa let the fire go out, not to have any accident, and they all went to bed. How The Eyrie shook and creaked in the gale! There was no rain, just whistling wind. It didn't hail, and there was no thunder and lightning. "It is not a hurricane," said Papa. It was just a huge great wind and nobody could sleep. From down below they could hear the great waves crashing, and Mama said, "Pity the poor sailors."

Bang! What was that?

"My sainted aunt!" said Papa. (This was an expression Papa had learned in his youth in Boston.) "That little porthole window upstairs! It's been open all these days. I just plain forgot to close it."

The window banged back and forth, opening and shutting. "Who'll go up and lock it?" Papa asked. "I better not on account of my foot. But we can't have that banging going on all night."

"I will," said Jerry.

"Isn't he brave!" marveled Rachel.

There was a curious rasping noise in the eaves. Mama said, "Oh, goodness! I suppose either some precious belonging of Mrs. Pulie's is being blown out, or some awful thing is being blown in. Hurry, Jerry!"

Jerry climbed up the same way Rachel did when she put Uncle Bennie's crickets up there. First he put a chair on a table. Then he climbed on the table and next the chair, and then he pushed open the little swinging doors and crawled into the alcove in the eaves. The doors closed behind him, and the people below heard him creeping along the floor of the little storage room and to the window.

The wind sounded ferocious, and Mama said, "Hurry up, Jerry! Goodness!" She wanted everyone to be close to her and for none to be in an eave. Then she hummed a little tune, trying to sound lighthearted.

Finally they heard the little window bang shut as Jerry closed and fastened it.

In the eaves, in the uncertain light cast by his flashlight, Jerry had a feeling eyes were on him. *Uncle Bennie's crickets,* he thought. And he had to laugh because he thought that crickets and grasshoppers have the funniest faces of anything in the world, they and goats. Of course he never said this in front of Bennie, who was just crazy about crickets. But to him they were funny-looking. He crawled back to the little doors and pushed them open. For a minute he sat on the ledging, and pushing his head out between the doors and dangling his legs down in space, he made funny faces at the family below.

"I'm a cricket," he said, trying hard to look like one.

Uncle Bennie, who had got out of bed to watch, blinked, for, in the darkness behind Jerry, he thought he saw, for just a second, two bright, round yellow eyes. Then they were gone.

"I never knew crickets had eyes that big!" he said. But no one heard him in all the racket of the storm.

Pinky and Gracie, the little and the big cat, sitting side by side down below, were engrossed in watching Jerry. They had, in fact, been mesmerized by Jerry's entire performance, his going up, his disappearing inside, and his trying to look like a cricket now. Gracie's smug face had an expression that looked as though she were saying, "I know something." Pinky's was dark and secretive.

Ginger whined and moaned. He did not like Jerry being someplace that he couldn't get to.

"Come down, Jerry," said Mama. "Ginger is so excited."

With the wind roaring, Ginger whining, waves booming, the noise was becoming nerve-racking. So Jerry came down, and Ginger licked his face anxiously as if he had been gone a long time and on a long journey.

"I hope nothing was broken up there," said Mama. "I did remind you about that window, didn't I?" said Mama to Papa.

"Never listens," said Rachel tolerantly of Papa. "Just never, never listens."

They all went back to bed. Pinky sat at the foot of Rachel's cot from which she could just barely see the swinging doors in the eaves. She studied them thoughtfully. Gracie sat at the tip end of Mama's bed, and she too slyly eyed the eaves. It was a long time before anyone could get to sleep in such a howling noisy wind as this.

Uncle Bennie began to suck his thumb. Every night he tried to not suck his thumb, but every night there was a reason for him to have to suck his thumb—robbers of kittens, broken ankles, wind, something. He had managed to give up pulling on Bubbah, his old piece of blanket that he liked to tickle his nose with while he was sucking his thumb. He had given Bubbah to his littlest bear for keeps. But he had decided one thing at a time, and he still sucked his thumb.

What a foolish thing to have done, to have given Bubbah to his bear! Just before the walk in the fog, "Here," he had said to his bear. "Here's my Bubbah for you, for keeps." How could he have known there was going to be this cyclone tonight and that he would need Bubbah badly? He got out of bed and ran to his big sister's room and climbed into her bed. She didn't mind. Soon, cozy and warm, he went to sleep.

The next thing he knew it was beautiful, broad, sunny, slashing daylight, and one by one everybody was waking up. The high wind had died down and there was not a cloud in the deep blue sky. The air was so light and buoyant, it was a wonder no one could really fly.

Uncle Bennie could not wait until after breakfast to have Rachel climb up and get his singing crickets. He wanted to see if they felt as happy as he. So, Rachel climbed up to the eaves.

Again the two cats lined up and watched with fascinated concentration, and they did not wink oncc. Rachel remained quite a while.

"Well," she said when she finally stuck her head back out. "There is not a sign of one of your crickets or grasshoppers or whatever they were in the box. Not one is left!"

"Oh-h-h," wailed Uncle Bennie. "Sams!"

"Probably blown away in the cyclone," said Mama. No matter how often Papa said there hadn't been a cyclone last night, just a great big blow, Mama insisted on calling it cyclone. Wind that was that big was more than just plain wind, she said. It was cyclone, typhoon, hurricane, or something.

They never had that kind of plain wind in Cranbury, she said.

"Vanished in the storm," said Rachel dramatically. She held the little apartment house of the crickets in her hands. It was curiously mutilated and battered. It looked as though pins had been stuck in it.

"Well," said Uncle Bennie resignedly. "I'll have to catch some new ones."

9

More about Grasshoppers

On the day after the big blow the children went down to the beach early, not to go swimming, but to see what sort of waves there would be on a day like this with air so light they could practically float down the dune. And they saw a marvelous sight. The waves were as high as mountains and burst with a great white spray upon the sand. The sky and the ocean were a deep, clear, unbelievably beautiful blue. And all up and down the beach they saw enough driftwood, boxes, wooden poles, and logs to make not one but, if they wanted to, a dozen wagon taxies. They made a beeline for one large and marvelous deep wooden box. It looked like an old chest that had once held pirate gems and gold.

Jerry also found a handle of a shovel, perfect for the handle to his wagon taxi. "You know," said Jerry. "Some sailor may have clung to this. Perhaps it saved some sailor's life. It could have, you know."

“I know,” said Rachel, awestricken and surveying the beach for a blue-clad, half-dead, staggering sailor.

The children plodded home with their finds, the big box, the shovel handle, and other prizes. Pinky was sitting on a windowsill, one paw daintily holding the thin curtain aside, and she watched the children with a welcoming, happy look. The effect of her bright pert face in the window was what she had expected. “Aw-w-w,” they said. “We ought to have a picture of that.”

Jerry set right to work on his wagon. *Bang! Bang!* The sound of his hammer echoed in the clear and sparkling air. Though Ginger did not like the noise and jumped every time the hammer struck, he remained loyally at Jerry's side. The big weather-beaten box fitted perfectly on the baby carriage wheels that Jerry had brought from across the bay. By noontime Jerry had built the best and roomiest taxi on the beach. He printed his name on it in clear deep blue letters, JARED PYE. Jared was Jerry's real name, and it looked better on a taxi than Jerry, which might have been confused with Berry and would then have given Touhy Tomlinson endless opportunities for teasing. "Hi, Berry!" he'd say. "What kind of berry pie did you say your name is? Blueberry Pye? Oh. Just Berry Pye." Jerry shuddered at the thought and made the JARED extra dark blue, to stand out.

In addition to being the best taxi for meeting boats, Jerry's taxi was a fine one in which to pull Rachel and Uncle Bennie. And sometimes the two of them could pull him. It was so deep Uncle Bennie almost disappeared inside. All you could see were his eyes. So Jerry put a small movable box in the front of it for the riders to sit on. Sometimes Jerry tied a rope around his waist for reins and pretended he was a pony. Sometimes he galloped very fast and sometimes he stopped short and wouldn't go at all, so Uncle Bennie had to crack the whip and make him giddyap.

Mama clasped her hands with joy at the idea of Uncle Bennie being carried around in a wagon. She thought now he would keep out of the poison ivy. The little twins in their peppermint-striped suits had waded in the poison ivy. "See? We don't get it," they said to Uncle Bennie. But after a while they did get it. "No, we don't care," they said. They didn't seem to feel anything, mosquito bites, poison ivy, or sunburn. And when the ocean was so cold that everyone else was frozen from the hips down, they said, "No, it's not cold."

Uncle Bennie had stopped caring about poison ivy too for a while, and he would hardly get rid of one patch when it would crop out somewhere else, so he began to care again. He was getting scared to touch any flower or shrub or even to pet Ginger or Pinky because, although they could not get poison ivy themselves, they could give it to him; and he was really getting tired of poison ivy.

"Stay in the wagon as much as possible," Mama urged Bennie. "What a nice wagon! Think of all the driftwood you can bring home in it for the fireplace. And when we go to the beach, we can pile it high with sweaters, and towels and things."

"O-o-oh," groaned the children. "From now on we'll take everything, just everything."

Sometimes Mama took even their winter overcoats to the beach in case the wind should shift suddenly and they should shiver. "With Jerry just over the measles and all . . ." she would say firmly when the children protested.

"I'm not just over the measles," said Jerry. "The measles were in May and now it is July."

"Just over," said Mama firmly. "And besides, have you counted the number of times we really have used everything we brought with us? And I can bring *War and Peace* to the beach now, too."

"What page are you up to?" asked Rachel. There were 1,111 pages in this book.

"Thirty-nine," said Mama. "Last summer I was up to there, too, but this summer I'm going to finish it."

Today Uncle Bennie said he was not going to the ocean with the others, so there would be a little less to carry. He was tired of the old ocean. It was too big. He had said to the waves, "Waves, stop a minute!" But they hadn't. He was going to stay home and catch crickets to replace the ones that had got lost in last night's blow.

He scarcely said good-bye when the others left. He was on his stomach, wiggling toward a black cricket, who was surveying him with a surprised and puzzled look. She was still more surprised a few minutes later to find herself scooped up in Uncle Bennie's warm little fist. "Sing, cricket," begged Uncle Bennie. This cricket did not sing, and it never did sing. It was the first nonsinging cricket that Uncle Bennie had caught.

"If it does not sing, it is a lady cricket, for lady crickets do not sing," observed Papa from under his green umbrella.

"Oh, yes they do," said Uncle Bennie. "Some do. Mine do."

"Never heard of that kind of a lady cricket," said Papa, and he went on stroking Pinky under the chin.

Pinky was purring, absentmindedly, like an engine unwinding, going more and more slowly, then, putting on steam, going faster again. Her eyes were fastened on Gracie, who was sunning herself on the little roof over the front porch; and Gracie's eyes were glued to the little round porthole window over the porch. In fact, all day long, not even coming down for lunch, Gracie had been staring into the little window over the porch. You would think she'd turn around the other way and get a view of the world. But her world was straight ahead and through the window into the alcove under the eaves. Now and then the tip of her tail twitched.

No one except Pinky noticed these telling signs about Gracie. But Pinky noticed them and she was puzzled, and that was why she forgot, now and then, to purr. The tip end of her tail twitched in answer to

Gracie's, for, without opening their mouths, cats talk to each other with the tip ends of their tails, which are very much like signal flags.

By the end of the day Uncle Bennie had managed to catch three new pets, two crickets and one grasshopper. This was quite a big haul for one day, and around the supper table everyone congratulated him. The peppermint-striped twins came by and looked at them stolidly. "Two are ladies," Uncle Bennie said to them. "For they do not sing."

"We know," they said. "You don't have to tell us," and off they marched to get cones.

Uncle Bennie had fixed up a new little apartment house for his crickets, a three-room house, and each captive was in its own room, broodingly poised on the grass Uncle Bennie had picked for its bed. After supper Rachel helped Uncle Bennie catch a ladybug for each and a lightning bug for each, so there was no favoritism despite the fact only one cricket could sing. It had a nice chirp, and it would have been easy to be fonder of that one than of the others that did not sing. Uncle Bennie tried tickling the backs of the nonsingers, with a piece of straw, which Papa said was the way the boys in China got their crickets to sing. But the nonsingers remained silent, so Papa must be right and these two were ladies and ladies do not sing.

Uncle Bennie and Rachel punched a few holes

in each room of this apartment house so the crickets could breathe and a very small hole between each room so, if any one of them wanted company, he or she could get a peek at his or her neighbor and say "Hello"—a silent hello from the silent ones and a chirped hello from the singer. They put the chirping one between the two silent ones, out of fairness and for better balance. The holes between the rooms were not so big that the sight of their neighbors would make them mad and they would tear the house down and eat each other up.

It was a neat little house, and the next day Uncle Bennie planned to paint it red. He put water in three tiny tin plates with fluted edges that had come with candy in them from the penny store, and at bedtime Rachel climbed up on the table and then up on the chair that was on the table; she pushed open the little swinging doors and shoved the house full of crickets in. They were safe from cats and dog and, with the little window closed, no heavy blow could blow them away.

Everyone went to bed, and it was sweet in the eventime to hear the sound of the singing cricket; a sweet and lonely song he sang. It is true he stopped rather abruptly. But what singer on earth does not stop singing abruptly now and then? Perhaps this singing cricket caught sight of his neighbor eyeing him through her little peephole, and this made him uncomfortable instead of happy. Perhaps one of the ladies said, "Keep still, can't you?"

He may have stopped for a drink, who knows? thought Uncle Bennie, comfortably settling himself in his snug little bed and saying his prayers over again, not remembering whether he had said them yet or not. Was his thumb in his mouth? Yes. He had not quite finished giving it up. Rachel had encouraged him. She had said, "Uncle Bennie, if at first you don't exceed, try, try again. That is a famous saying that someone said once and now everybody says it." Ah, he loved Rachel.

"Good night, Rachel," he said.

"Ni-ite," she said.

The way she said it almost made Bennie cry. He did love her so. She loved him too and she loved his grasshoppers and his crickets. There was no one else in the family who helped him. When he needed a box, she got one for him. When he needed to put the crickets carefully, one in one room, the other in another, she helped him not to break their legs. And she did the big and important and hard thing of putting them into this high and safe place under the eaves, free from danger.

Free from danger?

Free from danger, indeed! "What happened to my three nice crickets?" wailed Uncle Bennie in the morning. When Rachel went up for the cricket cage, she found the lid of the apartment house off and the three crickets gone. Crickets do not have the strength to raise the lid of a shoe box and get out of their house. Uncle Bennie knew this. "Still," he said, "they might. They just might have said in cricket language, 'Yo heave ho,' and pushed. All together. And then they might have eaten each other up."

Rachel said this might be so, since they enjoyed eating each other up. But then where was the one, the last one, the fat one that had the two others inside of him? Or, her. Maybe the last one was a her and was silently sitting somewhere, full of other crickets; and though she had plenty to sing about, naturally she couldn't make a peep. Had to celebrate in silence.

This was a great puzzle, and after breakfast Rachel and Uncle Bennie sat down under the green umbrella to solve it. Pinky sat beside them and daintily sniffed the little apartment house, which needed many repairs. The floor was damp where drops of water had been spilled, and one might think this house had been in a miniature hurricane. There seemed to be more holes for breathing than Uncle Bennie had punched in it. But Uncle Bennie was not absolutely certain of this. After all, he was only just four and could not be expected to remember everything, not where he had punched every single hole.

"I have a good idea," said Rachel.

"What?" asked Bennie, who liked good ideas.

"Tonight, we'll put adhesive tape on the roof to keep it on. They'll never be able to get out then."

"All right," agreed Uncle Bennie. And then he said crossly to Pinky, "Will you please get out of my cricket house?" Pinky with her spindly, spiky legs was stepping daintily over the walls from room to room, smelling each little hole long and thoughtfully, crouching down in a sneaky way and peeking up at them. It is hard to think that the face of a kitten of that age could look wicked, but hers did. "Go away," said Uncle Bennie, giving her a little shove. She scratched herself and went away.

Uncle Bennie did not have very much luck that day catching crickets, but he did catch one handsome olive green grasshopper. Grasshoppers do sing, though not as charmingly as crickets. He put the grasshopper in his pet cage and this, all adhesive-taped down, Rachel put aloft.

In the morning—same story! No grasshopper!

"He's gone!" said Rachel. "Not a trace of him! And he certainly tore this house open to get out!"

"Is there an animal up there?" asked Bennie. "An animal that could eat them?"

"Oh goodness, no!" exclaimed Rachel, coming down quickly at such a horrid thought. "Just suitcases and big boxes are up there."

"Could Gracie get up there?"

"Oh, no. She just sits and sits on that little roof, and she can't get in because during the big blow Jerry closed the window. Besides, when the window was open, she never bothered your crickets. That bell around her neck keeps her from trying to bother anything."

"Maybe she gets up there in the middle of the night when she doesn't have her bell on," said Bennie.

"Oh, no," said Mama, who had overheard the conversation. "Gracie does not get into the eaves in the nighttime. Why, she sleeps on my feet, and I wake up if she even turns over."

Mama was a very light sleeper. Everything, just everything, waked her up. She said there were little rustlings up in the eaves, and these often waked her up. Papa said there were lots of cracks and crannies in little beach cottages such as this, and what Mama heard was wind rustling through these and they could be anywhere in the cottage and not just up in the eaves.

Then Papa did a hard thing, considering his lame foot. To satisfy everybody, he climbed on a stepladder and, pushing the door to the little alcove open, took a good long look inside. "Not a sign of anything in there," he said, and came back down, all hands of all the family lifted to help him so he would not break the other foot.

"Do you think Pinky (Pinky, hearing her name, alerted herself by opening her eyes and bending one ear) gets up there and eats my crickets?" asked Bennie.

And then he answered himself. "No. She doesn't. Because she is too little. They just get away, they do. They go to grasshopper land. When we are all asleep, they go. I saw a beetle go through a crack as narrow as nothing once. Probably crickets can, too. Through the cracks and crannies they must go."

Of course Uncle Bennie could not catch a cricket or a grasshopper every single day. But he did catch one almost every day, and every evening he had Rachel tuck its little house up under the eaves. Sometimes the cricket sang up there while the family was having supper, and they all said, "There's Uncle Bennie's cricket singing." This made Uncle Bennie happy and proud and brought tears to his eyes. It was a very pleasant thing to have cricket-singing in the eaves, whether there was a soloist or a chorus.

But in the morning the little cricket would be gone. Three apartment houses had already been ruined.

Uncle Bennie and Rachel were sad. Two other members of the family, though they were not grieved, were interested in the disappearance of the crickets.

One of these was Gracie. Partially hidden by the pale pink rambler roses she spent practically all her time on the little roof over the porch, intently watching the dusty window of the alcove. She moved forward as far as possible on the roof so her nose was plastered against this window, and occasionally she dozed in this odd position.

The other interested member of the family was, of course, Pinky, who studied Gracie with utmost earnestness. Though saying nothing, they communicated with each other frequently. The tips of their tails gave sudden twitches, and on occasion Gracie made a crunching sound with her mouth. Pinky, uncertain as to the exact meaning of the crunch, merely let her mouth hang open, showing its pretty pink lining.

"I know what it is," said Rachel. "The cats are thinking about the crickets and the grasshoppers we put up there, and they imagine they are eating them."

"Yeh. Drooling," said Uncle Bennie, and he went looking for crickets. He told himself the whole story of the disappearing crickets. He thought they just must have escaped through one of the wind crannies and gone back to their own country. Perhaps he was catching the same cricket every day. That was one reason he called them all Sam, not to confuse a cricket with a new name in case it was one of the escaped ones. He wished he could put a date on their stomachs the way one does on turtles. Then he would know for certain whether today's cricket was yesterday's or some other day's escaped cricket.

"I know," said Rachel, who was really allowing interest in crickets to be on a par with interest in birds right now. "We can tie a little colored thread around the cricket, and if it should get away tonight, we can recognize it by the color of its thread. If, tomorrow, we catch a cricket with a piece of red silk thread dangling to it, we'll know that it's today's, Friday's cricket." Furthermore, this would be final proof that Uncle Bennie's crickets did escape and were not the victims of some voracious animal, or of each other. Maybe the cricket would walk or hop on its little red silken leash, be a real little pet on a leash for Uncle Bennie.

When Uncle Bennie, after careful stalking, did catch a cricket, he held it carefully and delicately, not to hurt its wings or legs, while Rachel tied the red string around it. The cricket did not mind, and it did hop along for one or two hops; but it seemed confused, so Bennie put it safely in its little house.

In the morning the thread was there but not the cricket!

"He wriggled out! He wriggled out! Ginger does

that too, wriggles out of his collar. What smart crickets I catch!" said Uncle Bennie in admiration.

On the morning of the escape of the cricket of the red silk string Uncle Bennie decided to consult Papa. "Papa," he said. (Of course Papa was not Bennie's real papa, he was his big brother-in-law. But Bennie had the habit of calling him "Papa" since he called his own Cranbury father, who was far away across the sound, "Father.") "Papa," he said, "what do you think happens to my crickets and grasshoppers at night? I'm not innerrupping. I'm just asking you what you think."

Papa's hands were behind his head. He was lounging in his comfortable chair under the green umbrella. Pinky was on his lap and Rachel was standing beside him. All awaited the answer.

Papa's mind was apparently absent, for he did not answer. However, he may have heard, for he looked wise, beneficent, and thoughtful. His blue eyes wandered vaguely to the little roof over the front porch upon which Gracie was straddled, sunning herself, in rapt contemplation of the dusty little window. Maybe she was admiring her reflection.

Mama was hanging out the bathing suits. (One thing she hated was to put on a damp suit, and she gave all the suits a good sunning every morning.) She overheard Bennie's question. She thought he might be interfering with some important thinking going on this minute inside her husband's head concerning a bird, so she said, "Now don't bother Edgar, Bennie dear. We'll find out. Where are the twins? Why don't you run along and play with the children?"

"Oh, I stopped playing with children now I'm four," said Uncle Bennie, and he went off hunting crickets again, question unanswered.

"Do you think we could find a better place than the eaves to put the cricket house in, in the nighttime?" asked Rachel, following him.

They thought and thought, but no place below seemed safe for captured crickets, away from cats and dog, with the exception of the breadbox, and Mama said, "No," to that. "Don't want those roaches in the breadbox," she said indignantly. "And don't want them in any bureau drawers either, hopping out at me," she said, thinking bureau drawers would be the next suggestion.

"Roaches!" exclaimed Uncle Bennie. "They're not roaches, they're crickets, and they're pets."

"No," said Mama.

"We'll try once more in the eaves," said Rachel. "Once more. And we'll tie the thread a little tighter. Let's use blue thread."

So Uncle Bennie resumed his quest, and Rachel lay down on the sand, dropping the fine grains through her fingers. Pinky came and studied the falling sand with grave attention. Mama began to pack sandwiches because all, with the exception of Papa, were going to picnic on the beach.

Rachel worried about Papa being lonesome. But he could, if he wanted to, ride up and down the wooden walks in his wheelchair. He often did this, ringing his bell briskly when approaching a person, and sometimes he took Pinky with him. Pinky would post along beside him, her pink tongue hanging out like a puppy's.

At the end of each wooden walk there was a little platform. From this platform, steps led down the dune to the beach. Sometimes Papa wheeled himself out on one of these platforms, binoculars in hand, to sit there, see the family below, wave signals to them as to what time of day it was, and also study the birds if there were any to study. You would be surprised how many there really were, plovers, sandpipers, gulls, terns . . . others. . . . Papa could even picnic with the family. "Do you want cheese? Or ham?" they would yell up to him, and Bennie would be the messenger boy.

However, today, as on many other occasions, Papa preferred to stay at home, and with his typewriter on his lap, and Pinky, too, he would work, think, study, dream. With Pinky he was not lonesome, he told Rachel, who finally had the courage to ask him. He really liked just to stay at home and work. His complete study of the birds here and the exploration of a sunken forest he had been told about could wait until his foot was well. And that would be soon.

"All right," said Rachel, and she kissed him good-bye and ran to catch up with Uncle Bennie. He was carrying his little cricket cage with him. He had just caught a lovely strong little cricket, and he had to take him to the beach to show him the great and wide ocean.

Papa sat under the umbrella with his wobbly little table over his knees and with the typewriter on it. Pinky leaped on his lap, crying "Woe." Soon they began to play the typewriter game. Tap one key with one paw, catch it with the other. *Pul-ink. Pul-unk.* And then the real typing began.

When you think of it, it is probably because Papa injured his ankle that we have as many records as we do about this summer. *Pul-ink. Pul-unk.*

10

Cat Games

While the family was away at the beach, picnicking, picking up shells, what was being typed under the green umbrella by the typing team of Pinky Pye and Papa?

Meditations of Pinky Pye II, that is what was being typed.

CAT GAMES

Dear cats: Following are some simple games called Solitaire.

Game of Take Your Time
Game of Pencil Grab
Game of Pencil Hide
Game of Mouse
Game of Making Beds
Newspaper Game
Game of In and Out the
Bureau Drawers
Game of Half-Dead Mouse
Game of Closet Creeps
Game of Dog's Ears
Game of Fix the Eye
Game of Catch a Fly
Game of Faucet Drip
Game of Pretend Mouse
Game of Knock It Over
Game of Woe-Be-Gone Bird

These games, which are in most primers, are good training for the harder ones that follow:

1. The String Bean Game

a. This important game *has* to be played with someone.

b. Now. Go to the icebox, sit in front of it, say "Woe," and Pye, or whoever you own, will come. Pye will understand what you want, for you will have the eager string bean game expression on your face. He will open the door of the icebox and rummage around for the bag of string beans. While he is doing this, you leap into the air with wild enthusiasm. Show that it is almost unbearable for you to wait for him to locate Bean. When he finally has the crispest, longest, and greenest bean and you get a whiff of it, leap higher and higher in the air. Try and grab it out of his fingers.

c. Now. Crouch and wiggle. This means you are ready for the throw. Pye will raise his hand as if to throw, but he will not do this right away, for he hopes to catch you unaware. Of course smart cats are never caught unaware, but we like to let people think they are, for delusion and deception lend spice.

d. Now. He throws Bean. Tear after it as though you have been shot out of a cannon. People are always surprised to see how fast you can get going without having to gather speed. Never let speed get ungathered. Race after Bean, bring it back, and lay it at Pye's feet. He throws Bean again. Race after it again, and if it has gone around a corner, knock recklessly into a wall as you make the speedy turn. Pick it up and trot back with it. Do this again and again. "Hurray!" the people will exclaim noisily. "She retrieves like a dog!" What nonsense! Dogs retrieve like dogs—huff, huff, pant. Cats retrieve like cats and bring variety to the game.

e. Now. It is time for variations, not to let the game grow dull, and you may think up your own. I now hide Bean. Pye then gets down on his hands and knees and searches. As he goes crawling from cot to couch, picking up a corner of this rug, or, flat on his stomach, peers under the icebox, he is a ludicrous and absurd sight. Sometimes I sit and watch his antics. Sometimes I lie beside Pye and peer where he peers, pretend Bean is outwitting both of us. And sometimes, to add zest to the game, as he searches I go leaping madly from table to mantel to bureau and then, upside down, race along the underneath side of a cot. (This last is excellent for sharpening claws.) When, finally, Pye locates Bean, repeat all these maneuvers until Bean grows limp, falls apart and—you eat Bean up!

f. Comment: This game develops the ingenuity of the two-legged ones, who are always searching for things they cannot find.

2. The Game of Crouch and Leap

a. Now. When Pye is lying on his bed, resting, pensive, come sidling silently to the doorway. When just your head is peeking in, stop, fix him (see Primer) with your eyes, mesmerize him, wiggling and squirming.

b. Now. Leap suddenly from the doorway to the bed and land right on his stomach. Turn, jump off, and run madly away.

c. Now. When, after a while, Pye, recovered, is again resting, pensive, unsuspecting, brooding about the birds he watches but does not catch, repeat this creepy crouch and leap. Always remember the long stare, which is to alarm. (I know a cat who could stare eight minutes without winking—my mother.) Pye knows you are going to leap, but he doesn't know when. Though a little frightened of the long stare, he loves the game.

3. Cat Tag

a. Now. Come running wildly into the room. Tag Pye's leg with a paw, race away, slide a rug in a heap, and tear through the house. When Pye tags you, spit at him, leap sideways on all fours and, hissing and spitting, prance back and tag him again.

b. Now. After a while Pye will say he is tired and would like to sit and think. That's his deception. Just look up at him with nose pointed, nostrils dilated, eyes big, round, and innocent. He will find you irresistible and play again and again until the game is really over, that is, when *you* grow tired. Then, walk off, shake your paw in boredom, or clean it carefully, sit down, and look into space. "What does she look at so long?" someone may ask, stooping down, peering stupidly where you are looking in air. Must there be something to look at in order to look?

4. The Game of Hide and Hunt

a. Now. Get into closets, bureau drawers, boxes, trunks, suitcases, and find things. Run furtively with what you have found, looking as sneaky as possible, and get underneath something with it, peering right and left for enemies. Hide things. "What has she got now?" people exclaim.

b. Comment: It is incredible how much time people spend in looking for things. "Where are my glasses?" "Where is my pencil?" they ask a hundred times a day. So. The more we hide, the more they can hunt. I help in all ways I can, hiding pencils under carpets, smoothing the carpet back down for the deception, putting paper bags on top of someone's glasses, or a newspaper over a thimble.

5. The Game of Watching

a. Watching is one of the most fascinating and important of all games. This happens to be a house in which watching is held in high esteem.

b. Now. Watch. . . . (More later. The family comes.)

Uncle Bennie and Rachel were the first to arrive, hot, panting, and thirsty. "Don't run with that grasshopper!" said Rachel.

"I have to give him some tea," explained Uncle Bennie, racing into the kitchen. Pinky leaped off Papa's lap and, hissing and spitting, coming sideways on bouncy steps, she rushed at Rachel. She drew up stiffly before Rachel and then bounced away. "Aw-w-w," came the admiring, marveling, infatuated cry. "If we only had a picture of that!"

When the rest of the family came around the cottage, they had Mrs. Pulie with them. She had dropped by with some mackerel wrapped up in a newspaper, which she had brought the Pyes as a neighborly gesture. She was always doing this, bringing them some clams, a fish, or crabs that she or her husband had caught.

"Isn't she generous!" marveled Rachel.

After she had left, Papa glanced at the newspaper that had been wound around the mackerel. It happened to be *The New York Times* of a couple of days ago, an issue that somehow or another Papa had happened to have missed seeing.

"My sainted aunt!" exclaimed Papa. "Listen to this, Lucy! Are you listening?"

"Yes," said Mama. "I'm listening. *I* always listen."

"Well, listen then," said Papa. "What do you think has happened now to that little owl of Hiram Bish's. Well, it's lost at sea. That's what's happened."

"Well," said Mama. "I always did think a boat was a silly way to travel with an owl."

"Well," said Papa, "when you think of it, practically any way is a silly way to travel with an owl. But they had to get him to the zoo somehow."

"How did it happen?" asked Rachel.

"Well," said Papa, reading, "you remember that big blow that we had a few nights ago?"

"Will I ever forget it?" asked Mama. "That cyclone, you mean."

"Well, in that big blow, that little owl, it says here in the paper, was blown away, blown off the ship and into the wind and the sea. Hm-m-m. Happened right off Fire Island, it says. How could that be? Hm-m-m. SS *Pennsylvania* lost its bearings in the fog, and when the fog cleared, the ship was off the shore here. Wind almost blew it into shore! What a narrow escape for everybody!"

"Everybody except the owl," said Rachel. "Why wasn't it in its cage? How could it blow away?"

"It says in the paper that Bish's wife, Myra, wanted to go out on deck (she never could resist a storm, I remember Bish telling me), and she decided to take the little owl with her so he wouldn't be frightened all by himself down in the cabin. Of course she couldn't have realized what a very bad blow it was . . . until she got out on deck."

"I told you it was a typhoon or something," interrupted Mama. "I told you so."

"Well, anyway," said Papa ("You can read the whole thing for yourselves in a minute," he said, for Uncle Bennie's and Rachel's and Jerry's heads kept getting in his way as they tried to see the story), "the wind yanked the owl out of her hands and it disappeared into space. The poor Bishes! They were crazy about that little fellow. Fiercest-looking little thing for anything that small!"

"Maybe he flew to land," suggested Rachel.

"Not likely," said Papa. "He couldn't fly in a wind like that! Even if he had been blown to land, he couldn't survive, for he has been a pet all his life and wouldn't know how to find food. All his meals have to be served to him."

"Well," said Uncle Bennie cheerfully. "What's gone is gone. My crickets is gone. And his owl is gone. That's fair."

Rachel cut the owl story out of the paper, and even if it did smell of mackerel, she pasted it on page two of her bird scrapbook. So far, both pages happened to be about a pygmy owl, the same owl.

"Poor little Owlie," she murmured, looking at the picture of him on page one, all fluffed up and healthy and ready for his travels. And now where was he? Lost at sea. "Poor little Owlie-wowlie."

11

The Watchers

The next morning, early, Rachel decided to climb up on the little roof where Gracie always sat and see if she could make some sort of bird discovery from up there. The Pyes had been here all this time and she hadn't made a bird discovery yet and, so far as she knew, neither had her eminent father. It was time someone discovered something. Up on the little roof she could watch and she could think.

So up she went. She braced herself against the corner of the cottage and then hoisted herself up and onto the little peaked roof. She straddled this and then she saw what a wonderful view there was from up here of the ocean, of the family's comings and goings, of everything!

No wonder Gracie liked it up here! Trying not to displease her, for after all this was Gracie's place first, and edging away from Gracie's spot, which was as near the dusty porthole window as possible, Rachel looked down at her father.

There he sat, under the green umbrella. His field glasses were beside him and so were his notes and papers, anchored by rounded rocks so they wouldn't blow away. Papa did not look like an injured bird man who has broken his ankle. He looked like a real right regular bird man watching and working in his khaki clothes on an expedition. Rachel's heart swelled up with love for her father.

Just look at him, she thought. *Studies the birds though his foot is broken. It is like "the show must go on,"* she thought. *It is going on, Papa,* she said to herself. *Your little daughter, not so little anymore, soon to be ten, is up here now, on the rooftop and on the brink of a great discovery.*

Rachel had no idea what this great discovery was going to be, but she had a feeling that she would make it and that it would be great. With her back to Gracie and the porthole window, she raised her binoculars and took a long look at the horizon. A big ship was sailing by. *It must have been just about there,* Rachel thought, *where that big boat is now, that the awful wind snatched poor little Owlie out of his mistress's hands and flung him into the sea, right into the mouth of a whale, probably, or some other big, widemouthed, hungry fish.*

"Stop it," she said to Gracie, whose tail was as strong as a wired thong and hit Rachel in the back

now and then as they were doing their watching, one facing inward, one facing outward.

I watch good, thought Rachel proudly. *When there is something to watch, that is. But when there isn't something to watch, you watch and watch and soon there* is *something to watch.*

Rachel had the idea that wherever her father went he attracted birds to him by the stillness of his watching. When he was away on a far trip, she visualized him as always being surrounded by beautiful and extraordinary birds. Now, seeing her father seize his binoculars and turn them toward the dune, she did likewise. A covey of terns flew upward in a lovely formation, and then, like the bursting of a beautiful night-firework, they dispersed, dipping over the dune and out of sight.

Papa and Rachel both watched for a further display of loveliness and, none coming, they turned their binoculars upon each other and waved. Then each went back to his own watching, Papa to his near watching and Rachel to her far and distant watching, for she had the idea that her great bird discovery was going to be discovered far away. That was why she was up here, to see farther.

"Stop it," she said to Gracie, whose tail thwacked her again.

She had never seen her father do great watching, for she had never been on an expedition with him, not before this. She imagined that he could watch as well as a certain man she had once seen at the zoo, who had looked not to left nor to right, but just straight ahead at what it was that was being watched, in that case—a monkey.

Yes. The best watching that Rachel had ever seen had been watched by this certain man at the zoo, a keeper in a khaki suit. She and Jerry had run ahead of the family to get to the monkey house first.

When they got near it, they saw this man in the khaki suit, a keeper, sitting on the ground with his back against a tree and looking up into a large tree opposite him, not taking his eyes off it, hardly winking, not saying "Quiet" to them or "Sh-sh-sh," because he could not take his eyes off what he was looking at.

She and Jerry had stopped in their tracks and they looked up into the tree where the man was looking. They had that much sense—to do that and to not ask questions—and up in that tree they saw a bright-eyed little monkey who was looking down at the keeper eagerly and happily and scratching himself.

A few yards beyond their first looker they saw another looker, a keeper in a khaki suit, too. This one was standing so still he seemed like a tree, and he, too, was watching the monkey and hardly winking and not turning his eyes to the left or the right either.

Then, out of the side of his mouth, softly, and to give the impression that he had not spoken at all in order not to upset the looking beam that was going on between him and the monkey, the first man, the sitter, said, "Please go away."

The children knew he was talking to them, and without a word they backed off, not taking their eyes off the man because they had never seen anything like this watching in all their lives before, and it sent the chills up and down their spines, as though they were watching a policeman trying to catch an escaped robber. They stumbled over a gray boulder and almost fell into the arms of the real policeman of the zoo.

"Why are the men watching the monkey?" Jerry asked him. "Did he escape?"

"Yes," the policeman said, and would not explain how it had happened, so Rachel and Jerry had to figure it out for themselves.

"Probably," said Jerry as they walked along, "the first man opened the door of the monkeys' cage to feed them and this one monkey scooted out between his legs. You know, made a dash for freedom."

"Yes," said Rachel. "And probably now he's wondering what his next move should be."

While Rachel and Jerry were doing this interesting speculating, still another keeper came along with a tray full of delicious foods such as a peeled banana, a mango, some peanuts, a juicy slice of watermelon, a chicken sandwich on white bread—a lovely lunch, which he put outside the door of the monkey cage. He hoped to bait the monkey back to his cage with this tempting array. But the plan had not worked up till the time the Pyes had to go home. The lunch was just making all the other monkeys drool intolerably.

Probably never did get him back, thought Rachel now. *Goodness,* she said to herself. *I almost forgot what I was doing. Watching. If only I had something to watch! I bet I could watch as well as that monkey-watcher.*

Gracie's tail gave her another big thump. "Now, Gracie," said Rachel, turning around and shaking her finger at the big old cat, "you must be careful and not knock me off the roof. One lame ornithologist around here is enough."

Gracie gave no answer. Her watching was concentrated as usual on the little window, sooty and cobwebby. "What are you so interested in?" asked Rachel. "Uncle Bennie's grasshoppers? There aren't any up there in the daytime. You know they only sleep up there. In the daytime we take them down, that is, if any of them are left alive. You should know that."

Rachel edged nearer the window and took a look in herself. She saw nothing. "You are dreaming of your great rat-catching past, aren't you?" Rachel whispered to Gracie, who did not answer but shifted her position a trifle and gave Rachel a look that plainly meant, "Get away from here." Rachel then resumed her right position, patiently picked up her binoculars, scanned the dunes, and prayed for some odd bird. Imagine an ibis!

The watching of Rachel and Gracie was not the

only watching going on at this moment. Uncle Bennie, of course, was watching grasshoppers and crickets and their life in the sparse grass that was their forest. He was not interested in the watching of anybody else.

For a time Jerry watched only Ginger, and Ginger watched only Jerry and the peanut that he was holding above Ginger's head. Jerry was teaching Ginger how to count. "Bark once for one, twice for two," urged Jerry. He held up the peanut, Ginger's reward when he got his lesson right. Eyeing the peanut, Ginger gave five excited barks for number one, and he haggardly pleaded for the suspended peanut. "No, no!" explained Jerry patiently. "Just one bark for one, two for two. You know now, don't you?"

Uncle Bennie, crawling by on his stomach, paused to say, "My bears can count. 'Ooze, dooze,' they say. That's one, two." And he wormed away on his stomach, for that is the best way to catch crickets.

Exhausted from their lessons, Jerry and Ginger sat back. Jerry gave Ginger the peanut anyway, for trying, and then he began to watch Uncle Bennie do his clever stalking. Ginger gave a profound sigh and lay down, his head between his paws. But he didn't close his eyes and he didn't take them off Jerry because he wanted to be ready for whatever came next, another peanut, a word of love—"Good dog!"—a trip to the boat, a "finding things" jaunt, anything.

Mama called Pinky, whose attention was hard to catch she was so busy watching the watchers on the rooftop. Finally she heard and loped to the back stoop, where Mama fed her some of the best food in the house. She spoke endearing words to her and put the saucer down where the delightful aromas were wafted to Ginger's sensitive smelling apparatus. What succulent smacking noises Pinky made! Ginger gave one disgusted look, hitched his shoulders uncomfortably, and resumed his watching of Jerry. Now and then, however, without moving his head, he rolled his eyes in Pinky's direction and then surrendered his thoughts to a petulant analysis of Pinky and all cats.

"Oof!" he said loudly to register contempt.

"Now, Ginger," said Mama. "You leave kitty alone. You'll have yours later."

Pinky looked up and said, "Woe?" in her most bewitching style.

"Ah-h-h," said Mama lovingly, and went back in the cottage to watch her pot in hopes it would boil.

Not looking at Pinky, but thinking glumly about her, Ginger gave another contemptuous "Oof!" He wondered gloomily why cats can't be like dogs.

When Pinky had finished, she sat and gave herself a thorough bath. Then she sauntered over to Ginger and rubbed up against his head. "Gr-r-r-r," Ginger said. Pinky put her ear close to Ginger's head and listened to his rumbling as one puts one's ear against a telephone pole to hear the humming. "Gr-r-r-r," said Ginger again, more loudly and like the rumbling of thunder. Pinky nodded her head as though to say, "It is what I expected," and she scampered off.

Settling down on Papa's lap again, Pinky scrutinized the main watchers of the family, Gracie and Rachel, who were as busy watching as ever. The tip of Gracie's tail was twitching back and forth as if it were mechanical, and Pinky cogitated about Gracie.

At this moment the first toot of the eleven o'clock boat sounded, and all watching, except for that of Gracie, whose head nodded sleepily but who kept her vigil anyway, and of Pinky, who continued to puzzle about the old cat Gracie and her watching, ceased.

Jerry called Uncle Bennie and Rachel to hurry up if they wanted to meet the boat with him. He wanted to be the first wagon boy there and earn ten cents. He plumped Uncle Bennie into the wagon and they all raced for the ferry.

"Too-oot!" sounded the bustling little boat as it edged into the slip.

Meeting the boat was a favorite pastime, wagon business or not, and seeing who came over on it was a real pleasure, even though the Pyes never knew any of the people. Someday they might know someone.

This time there weren't many people on the boat, in fact there was just one man. *I hope I get him,* thought Jerry; and he lined up his beautiful taxi with the others.

Funny-looking luggage he has, thought Jerry as the newcomer hove it onto the dock. He had one battered valise and a huge gray thing that looked like an old quilt.

"Taxi, sir?" asked Jerry, who happened, of all the taxi boys, to be nearest to the man.

"Yes," said the man. "Taxi."

12

The Man on the Ferryboat

Now this one man on the boat, whose luggage Jerry happened to be lucky enough to get, turned out to be a curious one. Not curious in the way some small children are, asking a lot of questions. But curious because he turned out to be another bird man. Wasn't it a curious happenstance that not only their father, Mr. Edgar Pye, but also this new man, just arrived on the Fire Island boat, should both be men who studied birds?

Moreover, was it not curious that this one lone man on the boat who was a bird man like their father should turn out to be a bird man of whom they had heard? H. Hiram Bish (though they had never heard of the extra H. he had), a friend of their father's! The name of Hiram Bish was now a familiar one to them, and it had been only yesterday that Papa had read them the story in the newspaper that had been wound around the mackerel telling how this very man's little owl had been lost at sea, his pet pygmy owl.

How had Rachel and Jerry found out so soon that this man was another bird man and one whom they knew about? Just by looking at a person you can't tell whether he is a bird man or what. You have to find out, somehow. Well, Rachel happened to see a sticker on his valise, a sticker from the boat the SS *Pennsylvania,* and it had on it the name H. Hiram Bish, Department of Ornithology, University of the Great and Far West. Ornithology may be a big word to some but not to a boy and a girl who happened to have an ornithologist for a father. They knew that in simple language it meant birds, just birds. When the man wasn't looking, Rachel gave Jerry a kick and pointed to the label. He lowered the corners of his mouth, indicating, "I see, hm-m-m, ornithology, yes . . ." And he and Rachel exchanged a meaningful glance.

Are there enough birds on Fire Island for two bird men to study during the same summer? Rachel asked herself. Their father, in a wheelchair with a broken ankle, probably was not seeing the best of the birds. This man, with his two good feet and two good legs, would probably probe every nook and cranny of the island with his spy glasses and his optical lenses and his notebooks and get the whole thing down and send it in first to the men in Washington.

Out of loyalty to her ankle-broken father, Rachel said, "Not many birds on Fire Island. Just a tern here or there." She hoped the man would take the boat back when he heard this discouraging news.

"Ah, I see," said Mr. Bish. "But it's nice here, though."

"Ye-e-e-es," said Rachel in a tone she intended to have sound some-may-think-so, some-may-not.

Then she felt ashamed of herself. "It really is very nice," she said, "when you get used to it. I mean with the poison ivy and all, it's not easy to get used to it. But we did. And there really are plenty of birds to go around, plenty. Not as many as in Cranbury, perhaps . . ."

"Cranbury!" said the man. "Why, I just came from there! What do you know about Cranbury?"

"We live there," said the children, "if you mean Cranbury, Connecticut."

"Indeed I do. Why, when I got to New York, I ran up there to say 'Hello' to my friend Edgar Pye. Do you happen to know him? He wasn't there. The neighbors were out, and I couldn't find a trace of him."

For a moment the children were speechless. Here was a man who had just come straight from their own town, Cranbury, from their own house, their very own tall house!

"Did you see Dick Badger?" asked Jerry. "And Duke?"

"Not that I know of," said the man. "But do you know Pye?"

"Pye is our father," they said. "We are the boy and the girl of Pye." And to prove the point, Jerry put his finger on his name in blue letters on his taxi—JARED PYE. "And this is our uncle," they said, pointing to Bennie.

"Not Edgar Pye! Not here on Fire Island! What a coincidence! What an unusual occurrence! No wonder he wasn't in Cranbury if he's here on Fire Island! The famous Edgar Pye! My friend Pye whom I went looking for in the town of Cranbury, Connecticut! The great bird man! Is that your father?"

"The same," said Jerry modestly. "Our father is Edgar Pye, the bird man. I never heard of any other Edgar Pye, anyway. There may be others, but I just never heard of them," said Jerry.

The children could see that Mr. Bish was as amazed at finding that their father was Edgar Pye and that he was spending the summer here on Fire Island as they were that another bird man should happen to come to this island, which was so sparse in this branch of life. But after a while it seemed to the children that there had been enough exclaiming, and Jerry asked politely, "Where would you like me to take you?"

"We-ell . . . ," hesitated the man. It became apparent that the man did not quite know where he was going. Since this sort of case had never come up before in Jerry's short life as a taxi driver, he could

only wait, hoping that the man would hit on a plan and state a destination. Still the man hesitated.

Now all bird men are rather poor, to judge by their own father anyway, and perhaps this man did not have the ten cents necessary to pay for taxi service. So Jerry said to Mr. Bish, "If you'd like to carry the quilt—whatever it is—the trip will be only five cents." After all, since Jerry's father was a bird man, all other bird men should have reduced rates. It was too bad that one of his first customers had to be a reduced rate man, but that was life, wasn't it? All doctors had to give doctoring free to other doctors, he had heard. And perhaps this taxi ride should cost the man absolutely nothing. "In fact," said Jerry, "this first trip of yours to wherever you want to go will cost you nothing. Because you are a bird man."

"Well, fine," said the man amiably. "But where's the taxi?" Again Jerry pointed to his wagon, and Mr. Bish caught on. "Oh, you're the taxi man," he said. "I'm slow."

"Oh, that's all right," said Jerry. "How would you know that wagons are taxis here? Do you want me to put the quilt, if that's what it is, in? Or do you want to carry it?" Jerry thought it might have expensive equipment in it for the man's expedition and he might want to take special care of it.

"Well, let's put it in the taxi," said Mr. Bish. "It's just my sleeping bag. Careful of it, though. It does have something rather fragile in the middle of it."

Sleeping bag! thought Rachel, and exchanged an ecstatic look with Jerry. All her life she had heard of sleeping bags, and now here was one right in their own taxi. No wonder the man was taking so long making up his mind "where to," with all this wonderful space to choose from for sleeping in his sleeping bag. She and Jerry waited respectfully.

After a considerable wait the man said, "Well, what are we waiting for?"

"Ha," laughed Jerry self-consciously. "Nothin'," he said.

"Well, let's go," said the man.

"All right," said Jerry, and started pulling his taxi wagon. *Where to?* he asked himself, and then he quickly answered himself. *Why, to the beach, of course.* That's where a man with a sleeping bag would want to go and stake out the best and coolest place to spend the day and yet the most protected for the night. He knew just the spot, so off he went, leading the way to the nearest little lane that led down to the beach. Rachel was proud of her brother. She had recognized the dilemma he was in and saw that he had now rallied his thoughts and knew what to do.

They came to one of the little landings at the top of the gray weather-beaten steps, sixty-four of them in this case, that led down the dune to the beach.

"Well," said Jerry. "Here we are. I guess I'll leave the taxi at the top of the stairs."

"I'll carry the suitcase," said Rachel.

"And I'll carry the sleeping bag," said Jerry.

The man stood on the landing staring thoughtfully out to sea. He was blocking the way so the children had to wait for him to drink in his fill. "Right off there, Owlie got lost," they heard him murmur.

Jerry and Rachel turned a sad expression onto their faces out of deference to his grief. Then, thinking that that was enough, Jerry said, "Shall we go down now? I know the best place for your sleeping bag, sir," he said.

The man gulped. His Adam's apple went up and down. *Not choking?* thought Rachel anxiously. *No,* she answered herself as the man regained his composure.

"I tell you what, though," he said. "Before I bunk in, suppose you run me around to pay my respects to your eminent father. How'll that be? And we'll investigate that best spot of yours afterward."

"All right," said Jerry with a shrug.

Rachel was amazed. If she had been the man, she would have wanted to get settled for the night right now. She had looked forward to the man's unrolling this sleeping bag so she could see what a sleeping bag looked like. Their father didn't have one. On his trips he rolled up in moth-eaten khaki blankets.

They backed the taxi off the platform and led the man to their cottage. "The Eyrie," murmured the man as they turned into their yard. "My, my," he said. "What an appropriate name for a cottage of a bird man. Did Pye name it?"

"Oh, no," said Rachel. "Mrs. A. A. Pulie named it. She is birdaceous, too, though."

"She's what?" asked Mr. Bish.

"Birdaceous," said Rachel. "Yes. Birdaceous. She's also boldaceous."

"What does that mean?" asked Mr. Bish.

"I suppose it means bold, more than bold, bold-my-gracious," said Rachel.

"Well, come on in," said Jerry.

The man was in no hurry. He was taking in the whole house, its location, everything. "I see you have a cat," he said, looking up at Gracie, who was looking evilly into the eaves.

"Two," said Jerry. "That's Gracie; and Pinky's on Papa's lap."

"Gracie seems to enjoy her lookout," said the man briskly.

"Yes, but it's more of a look in," laughed Rachel. "She hopes to see a grasshopper."

"High-flying grasshoppers, if you ask me," said the man.

And around the cottage they all strolled.

Rachel ran ahead to give the word of warning to Papa. *Here we are,* she thought. *Here we have a visitor who came over on the boat. Just like other people. And when he goes, we will all stand on the wharf and wave our handkerchiefs and cry 'Good-bye, good-bye' after our eminent visitor.* She presumed he was eminent, since there had been a story about him in the newspaper, him and his owl. Or was it the owl who was eminent, it being the one that had disappeared? Anyway it would be touching to wave good-bye to him, owner once of the eminent owl of newspaper fame. But here he hadn't even really arrived and she was waving good-bye to him in her mind. Joy in having a visitor now outweighed her dismay over his being another bird man.

Papa was still sitting under the green umbrella, typewriter table, typewriter, and Pinky all still on his lap. He was looking blandly and vacantly out toward sea. There was a lot of typing on the page.

Often, out of deference to her father and to indicate her great and absorbing interest in everything pertaining to him and to his exploits, Rachel would glance at the page of learned works upon which he happened to be working and she would ask, "What does this say?" or, "What does this long word spell?" and nod knowingly when her father said, "It spells *Eupsychortyx.* It is a genus." "Yes," said Rachel, "a genius."

Now, glancing hastily over her father's shoulders, from habit, she read some of his "works." Well. . . . No words like *genus* or *Eupsychortyx* at all. And all rather badly typed. "Why can't dogs be like cats?" she read.

Rachel did not have time to ponder this statement. She nudged her father to rouse him from his glazed-eye sun stupor and survey of the sea and sky and to call his attention to the fact that someone beside Pyes was in the yard and slowly approaching the green umbrella. Papa looked up at Rachel with his slow, loving smile and then, hearing Jerry's squeaking taxi, turned around and took in the rest of the entourage.

"Why, bless my sainted aunt!" he exclaimed. "If it isn't Hi Bish from the San Bernardino Valley." Dropping Pinky, he hopped up to greet Mr. Bish. "Ouch!" he said, and sat back down again. He had forgotten about his foot.

The two bird men soon settled down for a good bird conversation. Rachel knew that grown-ups do not like to have children standing around, listening and gawking every minute. So, even though she was in the same bird field as her father and his visitor, she tiptoed away. It is not necessary to tiptoe on sand, but from habit Rachel tiptoed anyway.

Pinky said, "Woe," and leaped after Rachel. Then she said, "Woe," again, and made several little holes in the sand and sat tentatively in each one of them until she had made one that was just right and she sat in it like a little cat statue. "Not very polite," said Uncle Bennie, and he and Rachel and Jerry and Ginger went into the cottage to inform Mama of the arrival of the man on the ferryboat.

Mama saw nothing unusual in their being visited by a bird man whom they knew and yet who hadn't known that they, the Pyes, were here on Fire Island.

"Things like that happen all the time. They just do," she said.

She went out to greet their guest and to meet him, for he had never been east before and the farthest west that she had ever been was Hoboken. "Your wife didn't come?" she said.

"No," said Mr. Bish. "She is visiting friends in Washington. She is very upset over the loss of our little owl and blames herself largely for his disappearance."

"We read about your little owl," said Mama, "just yesterday in the newspaper that was wound around the mackerel. What a shame to lose him and in such a curious fashion!"

"Yes," said Mr. Bish in a low and solemn voice. "And right off this island of yours. Mm-m-m. That was some blow you had! Mm-m-m."

Mr. Bish had a way of saying "mm-m-m" at the end of sentences, and somehow this "mm-m-m" made the children feel guilty. It wasn't their island anyway, and it hadn't been their blow.

Mr. Bish sighed. "He was so little, Owlie was. He let us scratch his head. Looked fierce but liked us. Let Myra carry him around. We've had him since he was right out of the egg. He was a nice owl and a rare one that the zoo, which hasn't much in the way of owls, was very anxious to acquire. Mm-m-m."

The children listened attentively and respectfully.

Mama, after a polite pause, not wanting to change the subject in a second, even though it was a painful one, said, "Could you have luncheon with us? We'd love to have you."

Mr. Bish cleared his throat and said, why yes he could, if it were not too much trouble.

Glad to have a free meal, thought Jerry.

"That will be so nice," said Mama, going in and hoping that the man liked potato pancakes fried in diced bacon and served with homemade applesauce, which was the menu for today.

"Hurray!" said Uncle Bennie. "What a lunch!" He watched Mama grind the raw potatoes and marveled at the way they turned pink when the air hit them. "Why do they?" he asked.

"They just do," explained Mama.

"Oh, I see," said Uncle Bennie, nodding understandingly, and he hungrily sniffed the bacon sizzling in the skillet.

When luncheon was over (and did Mr. Bish go for those pancakes! "My, he certainly ate with great relish," said Mama privately and with satisfaction to Uncle Bennie. "May I have some sometime?" asked Uncle Bennie. "Some what?" asked Mama. "Great Relish," said Uncle Bennie. "Certainly," said Mama), all adjourned again, hoping the dishes would wash themselves. They sat under the green umbrella and listened to stories that Mr. Bish had to tell of his little pygmy owl.

"Did he like to be petted?" Rachel asked, imagining what a wonderful soft little pet a baby owl would make.

"No," said Mr. Bish. "He was a fierce little fellow. But he got so he let Myra pick him up. She was his favorite. But no one else."

"He'd let me," said Rachel confidently.

"He was awfully cute-looking and we were very fond of him, and he did like to have his head scratched."

"Woe," said Pinky, who was dreamily watching Gracie, who was, as usual, up on the little roof, turned inward, thumping her tail and staring.

The man on the ferryboat, as the children called him, stayed all afternoon, going for a swim with them, and so then he stayed for supper; and then he said he guessed it was time for him to find a place to sleep, mm-m-m. Mama said apologetically that although she would love for him to stay here in The Eyrie, they did not have an extra bed. Mr. Bish said that he was so used to sleeping in odd places on his bird trips that he did not mind sleeping on the floor in his sleeping bag, which he had brought with him.

Mama had been wondering what the grayish-looking object out on the porch was and was glad to have the object explained. She wondered, "Is it polite to let our guest sleep on the floor while all five of us and also Ginger and Pinky are sleeping on a bed, if we can sleep, that is, with worrying about the man's hard floor?"

The children were waiting with bated breath to hear what Mama would say, but before she could reply, Mr. Bish said that he had changed his mind and he had decided that, since it was a pleasant night, he would prefer to sleep in his sleeping bag down on the sand instead of on the floor. Jerry and Rachel had previously shown him the very spot.

Of course he would rather do that, thought Rachel ecstatically. *Who wouldn't want to sleep in sleeping bags under stars if one could?*

"Oh, come now, Bish," said Papa. "Sleep here with us. On Fire Island there's quite a heavy mist every night."

Then it seemed that Mr. Bish appeared to be willing to change his mind again, and he consented to sleep here rather than under the stars.

Well, he'd probably like a vacation from sleeping under stars or in a mist, a moist mist, Rachel reasoned.

Then it became quite apparent that Jerry would like to sleep in the sleeping bag. "You could sleep in my bed," said Jerry to Mr. Bish. "And I could sleep in your sleeping bag," he suggested.

Uncle Bennie wanted to sleep in it, too. "I don't take up much room," he said, watching delightedly as the man spread out the wonderful sleeping bag.

"This is my lost owl's cage," said Mr. Bish, removing it from its safe place in the middle of the bag. "I don't know why I brought it along. I just did, mm-m-m."

Uncle Bennie wanted to say that if the man did not need his cage anymore, his owl being gone, he, Uncle Bennie, would like it for his crickets and grasshoppers. Of course he knew it is not polite to ask for things, so he didn't say this out loud. But he certainly wished that his latest cricket, one that he and Rachel had ornamented with a pale blue thread, could sleep in the owl's cage—he in the man's sleeping bag, the cricket in the man's cage. That would be fair, wouldn't it? he said to himself. If the cricket could not squeeze out of the cage, that is.

Pinky smelled the cage delicately, thoughtfully, and she sat and pondered. Gracie smelled it, and she looked wild. Her tail twitched nervously, and she made an audible crunching sound with her mouth. "An old experienced cat, mm-m-m?" observed Mr. Bish.

When the sleeping bag was spread out, Uncle Bennie, having clean feet, crawled in. Pinky cautiously and curiously followed. The others had to laugh as her stiff little black tail disappeared within. "Woe." They heard her smothered cry as she encountered Bennie.

Ginger was also anxious to explore, so he and Jerry crawled in next. "I hope you do not mind all these intruders in your little house," Mama said.

Mr. Bish laughed. "There have been many less desirable intruders than these nice tame ones," he said ruefully, and described how once, in the desert, a lizard had crawled in. "We took him home to Owlie, and Owlie ate him up with great relish."

"Oh, couldn't I have Great Relish with my food too someday?" begged Uncle Bennie. This was the second time in one day he had heard of great relish, and it sounded good.

"Sure, sure," said Mama, stroking his sleepy, hot little face sticking halfway out of the bag.

"Well, can we sleep in the sleeping bag?" asked Jerry. "Please. That is, if Mr. Bish doesn't mind sleeping on a bed instead."

"Ah, not at all, not at all," said the man warmly.

"All right, Jerry," said Mama.

So it was arranged that Mr. Bish would sleep in Jerry's cot and Jerry and Uncle Bennie would sleep in his sleeping bag, the other members of the family sleeping as they always did. Mama hoped that this arrangement would be only for tonight, for she imagined she herself would not get much sleeping done with children on floors in bags. And Bennie would probably get too hot and catch cold, or else he would take up all the room so Jerry would not be able to sleep. And Jerry needed his sleep; he'd just got over the measles in May. Well . . .

Suddenly, to take them by surprise, for of course they had all forgotten she was still in it, Pinky thrust her pert little face out of the sleeping bag. "Woe," she said.

"Oh-h-h," they all gasped, hardly able to bear such adorable ways.

Uncle Bennie now got ready for bed, or rather for sleeping bag. He was rather shy in front of strangers like Mr. Bish, especially when he had on only his sleepers, so he crawled quickly into the sleeping bag. He made a desperate and victorious effort not to put his thumb in his mouth or the man might not let him, a baby, sleep in his manly sleeping bag. He breathed a sigh of bliss. To sleep always in sleeping bags! That was the way to give up sucking thumbs and pulling on blankets. He wished the man would stay all summer, all, all summer.

Finally everyone was in his respective bed. The Pyes felt as though they were visiting in another house, having this man who had come over on the boat staying with them, and with Jerry and Uncle

Bennie sleeping in this unusual style on the floor in a puffy sleeping bag.

Outside, the waves and the peepers made their usual sort of music; the breezes made gulping noises with the green umbrella, trying to carry it off; and inside, quiet settled over The Eyrie. But the quiet was that of nonsleepers, not of sleepers.

13

Listeners in the Night

On this first night of the visiting bird man's stay with the Pye family, no one, not those in the sleeping bag, not those out of the sleeping bag, could get to sleep. They tried. They tried all the ways they knew of for going to sleep, counting sheep, kicking off blankets, pulling up blankets (that was those out of the sleeping bag), groaning "O-o-oh" (that was those in the sleeping bag). Everyone tried to be quiet because everyone thought everyone else was sound asleep except himself.

Mama had begun to think about what kind of eggs people would want for breakfast. This kept her awake. She wondered if the man liked scrambled eggs for breakfast or what kind. She hadn't asked, for the man might not know the night before what sort of egg he would fancy in the morning. *I hope it's not omelette,* Mama thought, *because I'm not so good at omelette.* Her family always knew what sort of egg they preferred. Each one had an egg prepared in a different way. Rachel had a hard, hard fried egg. Jerry had a hard fried egg but not *quite* so hard as Rachel's and with just a very little of the yellow way inside soft. Uncle Bennie had his like an Easter egg, hard-boiled, and with a little mayonaise if possible. Odd for breakfast, but that's what he liked. Papa liked scrambled eggs. The cats and dog ate any sort of leftover egg with equal interest. Mama herself also liked any sort of egg. And whatever sort of egg Mr. Bish liked he could have. Probably every way of cooking an egg that she knew of would have to be put into operation in the morning.

Mama tried to count sheep in order to stop thinking about eggs, but she soon lost track and fell back on the eggs and hoped she would not be too tired to prepare a wonderful breakfast for their guest. After all, one needs a good night's sleep in order to fry one's best egg.

The clock struck eleven. How late it was! Mama began to worry about the sleeping-bag sleepers. Was that contraption warm enough? She should have crawled in and felt it. It was probably not warm enough for damp seashore life. If she got up and threw the old green comfortable on them, everyone would surely wake up, and in the morning what a lot of tired and grumpy people there would be! She listened hard to the quiet breathing and tried to count the breathers. The clearest breathing she heard was, naturally, that of her husband. But his breathing did not sound like that of a sleeper, it sounded like the breathing of a listener.

Mama liked the idea of his being awake. It was company for her, and if they had been at home instead of here, they could have had a nice conversation about something, like that time on the escalator. But what, she wondered, was keeping him awake? She hoped his foot did not hurt him. And then she thought she heard a rustle in the eaves. She had often, being a light sleeper, heard this sort of rustle in the eaves, and Papa had always said, "Wind in crannies." There wasn't any wind at all tonight; not a breeze was stirring and still there was a rustle. It must have been made by an escaped cricket of Uncle Bennie's. Uh! The house was probably full of escaped crickets! Why didn't they sing? The least they could do was sing.

Papa heard the rustle too and he listened as hard as he could, for next to watching, listening is probably the second greatest art of the bird man. But he didn't hear the rustle again. Seeing Gracie's gleaming yellow eyes slanted in the direction of the eaves, he, too, thought "cricket." *Must be one of the little fellow's pets,* he said to himself.

Papa had been feeling disconsolate, and his foot did hurt him, not much, but enough to keep him awake. Or perhaps the animated bird conversations with Hi Bish had aroused him so he couldn't go to sleep. They had been interesting, but they made Papa feel dissatisfied with himself. He had meant to accomplish so very much this summer. And so far what had he been doing? Nursing a sore foot and just sitting typing, with Pinky.

Well, Papa and Mama were not the only listeners in this cottage tonight, for it happened to be a night of hard listening for every member of the family, pets and all—even guest.

In their sleeping bag, which, in the beginning, had seemed to be such a marvelous idea, the boys were doing a great deal of tossing around. Each thought the other was taking up too much room and tried to shove the other over. Moreover, the floor was very hard and could be felt through the sleeping bag from any position. *Oh,* thought Jerry. *If only the man from the boat had taken a room somewhere like other people who come over on boats!* Mr. Bish could then have left his sleeping bag here for safekeeping, and Jerry and Uncle Bennie could have slept in it; but they could have slept in it on top of a soft bed. Then they would be in a sleeping bag and on a comfortable bed, both. And they would not be feeling all these boards in the floor of knotty pine.

The truth is he and Uncle Bennie were too much for this one single sleeping bag. Each of them should have one. And now here came Ginger. Not

content with staying at the foot of the bag where he belonged, he had to come up and lick Jerry's face; and then he noisily began to lick himself and, *thump, thump,* to scratch fleas. Jerry was embarrassed. How could the man sleep with such a racket? "Sh-sh-sh," he whispered. Finally Ginger lay down with his head between Jerry's and Uncle Bennie's, like another person.

Jerry wondered if Uncle Bennie was asleep. He probably was because little fellows fall asleep anywhere, on trolley cars, even standing up, anywhere. Hard boards are not enough to keep these little fellows awake. When it is sleep time, they sleep. And then Jerry heard a soft and curious-sounding rustling noise somewhere in the cottage, and he wondered what that was.

Now of course this curious rustling sound that Jerry heard was the same sound that Mama (one), Papa (two), and Gracie (three) so far have heard. In fact, every member in the cottage heard it, but we can take them up only one at a time and we are now up to Jerry, who is the fourth. In the opinion of Mama and Papa, arrived at separately and silently as we know, the rustle was crickets, just plain crickets. In the opinion of number three, that is, Gracie, it was . . . ? Jerry (number four) thought it was just the soughing of an old beach house. Ginger (number five) thought it was something, not dangerous exactly, but unusual; and he let out a small "oof!" Jerry throttled the oof before it became two oofs, so it sounded as though Ginger were having a nightmare, and with his feet he pushed Ginger back down into the bottom of the sleeping bag.

Now we are up to Uncle Bennie, who is number six of the nonsleepers, the listeners, and the hearers of the rustle. Uncle Bennie was not able to go to sleep. Contrary to what Jerry supposed, little fellows on the order of Uncle Bennie do not go to sleep just anywhere. They may on trolleys and trains, but sometimes they do not just fall right to sleep when they are in a sleeping bag. Uncle Bennie was the type of little fellow who stayed awake because sleeping in a sleeping bag is a rare and exciting thing to do and not to be compared with trolleys, on which he rode several times a week.

The funny thing was that he had been so sleepy before he got into the bag. But the minute he got into it, he was wide awake. He began to think about his thumb. He was proud of himself because he had not sucked his thumb once the whole day and not, so far, tonight. Who knows? The day the man came over on the boat and the night that he, Uncle Bennie, slept in a sleeping bag, might end once and for all his sucking of his thumb. And that wouldn't be so bad, would it, to give it up two weeks after his birthday instead of right smack on his birthday? *Better than nothing,* he thought, and put his thumb in his mouth for old time's sake. And then he forgot to take his thumb out because he heard an unusual noise, and it was not the noise of Ginger scratching his fleas either, it was a rustling sound and it was up in the eaves.

There goes my cricket! said Uncle Bennie to himself. He was so excited, he wanted to yell to Rachel to wake up and hear the going-away of his cricket. There was his newest blue-threaded cricket getting away, making his clean getaway. The escapes of all the crickets and grasshoppers had been clean. They had left no mess after them; they had disappeared entirely and joined their brothers and sisters somewhere. There were always sharp little bites on the cricket boxes in the morning. But if a cricket can fight another cricket so hard that he can kill it, then a cricket can bite a cardboard cage and escape. Uncle Bennie was sure that his crickets escaped and that they had not been attacked by anything else alive up there. Rachel said she had examined the alcove thoroughly, and she could find no signs of squirrel, chipmunk, or mouse. She said Mrs. Pulie must have had a great fondness for seaweed, for there was an awful lot of that, all dried up and in corners. Maybe the crickets were living in that. But Uncle Bennie could not expect Rachel, who did not have his terrible fondness for crickets, to shake out the seaweed, examine it, and see if they were.

Uncle Bennie concluded that his crickets were amazingly clever to think up such good escapes, and this explains why he continued to put his crickets up in the alcove so trustingly. To those who asked, he said, "I keep putting my crickets up there because they have a secret place they get away to, and when I have caught a captain for them, they are going to have a simfiny awkstra." Uncle Bennie listened. The rustling gradually ceased. He was getting free, right then, that's what he was doing, thought Uncle Bennie. "Good-bye, cricket," he whispered, a little sadly.

Ginger remained awake. He knew that the cats were awake and he knew the whole family was awake, and when he heard that rustle in the eaves, he gave that little "oof" to let them know he was on the alert, even though he was in this uncommon spot down on the floor in a sleeping bag, and to let them know that it was not a very important noise but that he would study it and remain on guard.

He didn't have to oof, thought Pinky in disgust. *We knew he was awake.* She and Gracie exchanged a glance that was full of disdain. "They oof and what is the sense of it?" they asked each other silently, for cats can talk to each other without saying a word. Sometimes a cat a block away knows what a cat in your house is thinking. And Gracie and Pinky went on with their silent contemplation of the closed swinging doors to the eaves. For a while, after the rustle, the tips of their tails thumped the covers hard—*bum, bum, bum.*

Of course it wasn't Ginger's oof that had waked Rachel, for she, too, number seven of the nonsleepers, was awake already. The reason she couldn't go to sleep was because she wasn't in a sleeping bag. She felt excited. You would think it was the night before Christmas and Santa Claus in the chimney. She must be excited because with the man from the ferry-boat in the house and with a sleeping bag here too, this night became a different sort of night, almost as exciting a night as that of the big blow. That night this man from the ferryboat had been on a big boat, little Owlie with him. This night he was here, alone, little Owlie gone!

Rachel had a habit of putting herself to sleep at night making speeches. But she couldn't lose herself in her thoughts tonight because of the excitement. Besides the excitement, her ankle itched. Probably now she had poison ivy. "Oh, to be in a sleeping bag!" she groaned. "A sleeping bag is probably like a sleeping pill. The minute you get in the bag, you probably fall asleep. Oh, let the man from the boat," she prayed, "spend tomorrow night here too, and then I will have a chance at it. Pinky would like to sleep in the sleeping bag too, wouldn't you, Pinky?" she addressed the kitten silently.

As if she knew that Rachel was thinking about her, Pinky kissed her with her cold little wet nose. She had a very endearing way of butting her cool little mouth against yours, as though bestowing a number of gentle kisses. Then Rachel, number seven of the listeners, and Pinky, number eight of them, heard this same rustling that all the other listeners had heard. Pinky's tail twitched back and forth mechanically, batting Rachel on the head. "Don't," whispered Rachel. *"Ts." That was probably Uncle Bennie's cricket going, going*... she thought.

Pinky, like Gracie, thought the rustling sound was . . . ?

The sound of the peepers welled up and filled the whole world with their shrill and sad and mourning song. *It's those peepers that are keeping me awake,* thought Mr. H. Hiram Bish, number nine of the nonsleepers. Mr. Bish was used to mockingbirds in the night, not peepers. He turned over on his squeaky cot as softly as possible in order not to awaken any of the other people, the very nice and hospitable people of the Pye family. He fell to considering the strange sequence of events that had led him to Fire Island, which had not been on his program at all.

First, the boat trip from California with his wife and their little owl; then the ill-fated night of the great blow that had carried Owlie off the boat; then his fruitless visit to Cranbury to say "Hello" to his brother ornithologist, the noted Edgar Pye; and then, just this morning, he had been in Pennsylvania Station and about to take a train and rejoin his wife, who, instead of going to Cranbury with him, had gone on to Washington, and what had he done? Instead of boarding the train for Washington he had hopped on one for Fire Island!

Curiosity, I suppose, he mused. *It's a curious name and I had never heard of it until that night on the ship. So now, here I am, on it, on Fire Island with—of all people—the renowned Edgar Pye. Imagine my finding Pye here! Just by luck. For supposing one of the other wagon boys had got me instead of Jerry? Then I should never have known that Pye was here. But such strange whims of fate are the warp and the woof of our lives,* he thought. *To think that right off this island of Pye's, little Owlie was last seen, whirling mad-eyed and terrified into the roaring wind. Probably dashed into the ocean, poor little fellow,* thought Mr. Bish disconsolately. He had been very fond of the little owl.

Of course Mr. Bish heard the rustle in the eaves, too. But he just didn't think anything about it one way or another. He was not as familiar with the cricket story as the others were, and he just thought, *New places, new sounds.*

Again the sound of the peepers seemed to swell higher and higher through the night air. But the listeners in the night, one by one, at last became sleepers in the night. Ginger gave a sigh, smacked his lips, and went to sleep. The last to give in were the cats. Gradually their tails stopped twitching. Their little faces sank between their paws. The final thought of Pinky as she fell off to sleep was, *Why do dogs have to sigh? Why can't they be quiet about going to sleep? Like a cat. Not proclaim everything to the world, show every feeling.* Her tail gave the bed one last thud. She said to herself, *Remind me.* (She had fallen into many of Mr. Pye's ways of speech.) *Remind me, I must get up to the eaves tomorrow.* And so resolving, with no sighs, not one little "woe," she slipped off to sleep.

14

The Ascent to the Eaves

In the morning, after everyone had had their eggs the way they wanted them, and Mrs. Pye was right, that was in six different ways, each person marveled at how strange it was he didn't feel one bit tired after staying awake half the night. For in comparing notes at the breakfast table, each one confessed that he had not slept well. Rachel was astonished that the sleeping-bag boys had not slept. Perhaps they had not been in it right. Uncle Bennie claimed he had not slept at all. He had heard his crickets and his grasshoppers rustling about in their secret hiding place in the eaves. One cricket sang, he said. At least he thought he had heard one cricket sing.

This reminded him and Rachel of his blue-threaded pet, so Rachel went up to the eaves to get it and, of course, it was gone. All remembered then about the rustle, and all agreed they had heard the cricket escape except for Mr. Bish, who had not had crickets on his mind. The story of Uncle Bennie's crickets and grasshoppers had not come up yesterday or, if it had been touched upon, it had not been gone into very deeply. The Pyes went into it now, a little bit, and for a while Mr. Bish was very interested. Then his face grew pensive as he thought of the nice green grasshoppers he used to feed his dear Owlie in the old days before he had been lost at sea.

After breakfast Mr. Bish said he would like to explore this island. (To tell the truth, he secretly hoped against hope to find Owlie somehow, somewhere, even though common sense told him Owlie must be dead.) Papa said that down at Point o' Woods, a nearby little settlement, there was a sunken forest that was considered to be one of the most interesting sights hereabouts.

Mr. Bish said he would like to go there. This was too far for Papa to wheel himself in his wheelchair or to hobble to on his broken foot, so he would have to stay home. The rest could go though, he said. But when Mama saw how swollen one of Rachel's ankles was, she said that Rachel would have to stay home too and keep off it. To Mama, Rachel's ankle did not look as though it had poison ivy. "Probably sand-flea bites," she concluded.

"Ezzackly what is a sunking forest?" Uncle Bennie asked. "How do they know it's there if it's sunking?"

Rachel wanted to know, too. "I've heard of a lost

river," she said. She visualized a river flowing along peacefully, winding in and out of a gentle countryside, and then going right down into the earth; or else a swift river racing madly down a mountainside and suddenly going underground, becoming "lost." That would be an unusual thing to see and so would a sunken forest.

But no one could tell her or Bennie what a sunken forest was because no one had seen it yet. Rachel was disappointed not to be going to see it. But Mama said all of them would go later in the summer when the people with the hurt feet got well.

"Well," said Rachel to her father. "We'll both stay home this time, you and me, and we might discover a bird discovery right at home."

"We might," said Papa, puffing pensively on his pipe.

Rachel thought, *He's dreaming about all the great birds he's missing and that Mr. H. Hiram Bish, the other bird man, will probably see today.*

It took Mama quite a while to get everything in order for the expedition. "I can carry it all in my wagon," offered Jerry. "We'll go at low tide and it will be low again by the time we come back, so I can easily pull the wagon on the hard sand."

"Fine," said Mama. "And if Uncle Bennie gets tired, he can ride too."

"Tired!" yelled Uncle Bennie. "I never get tired."

"'Be prepared' is my motto," said Mama, smiling at Mr. Bish, who was looking with astonishment at the equipment for the safari. It probably was as much as he would take with him on a major trip. "Perhaps we should take your sleeping bag," said Mama. "In case anyone needs to sleep. Oh, matches, too," she added. "Haven't you read of people going into forests, they may not have been sunken ones but they were forests all the same, and the people would have been all right if only they had remembered to bring along a match? In case of cold, you know, and you have to make a fire," she explained, tucking some in her bag. "Now. Is everything ready?" she asked. "You two won't be lonesome, will you?" she asked, stroking her husband's forehead and peering anxiously at Rachel's foot.

"Oh, no," said Papa. "I have Rachel and I have Pinky, not to mention the great New York cat on her pedestal." Gracie, hearing her name, cast a suspicious glance downward and then resumed her scrutiny of the eaves.

And Rachel said, "And I have Papa and Pinky and the great and famous New York cat."

Even so Papa did look a little lonesome sitting under the green umbrella, his foot projected before him and his portable typewriter on his lap; and so did Rachel, who, taking along the *Green Fairy Book* for between birds, had swung herself expertly to her little spot on the roof that really belonged to Gracie. Good-byes were waved both by those on safari and by those at home. "I've left your nice lunch in the icebox in wax paper," said Mama, and turning away from the lonesome sights of Papa under the umbrella and Rachel on the roof, she put a brave smile on her face, and off the sunken-forest party went.

Held captive in Papa's lap so she would not follow, as she often did, and with Papa murmuring enticing promises such as "string bean game" and "typing" in her ear to keep her satisfied (Papa didn't know that Pinky had a plan or he need not have bothered), Pinky yawned and stretched. Then she gave her little white paw a thorough cleansing, for she was very proud of this paw and kept it in a sparkling condition. Sometimes she stuck just her white paw out from under the sofa, and people would say, "Oh, I didn't know you had a white cat." After polishing this paw tidily, Pinky settled down for a little nap on Papa's lap. She had not forgotten her resolve to get up into the eaves today, but she had studied the situation, and noting that right now Gracie was dozing and that her tail was not twitching, she knew that the moment for her bold venture was not quite here. She put her little head down on her two paws, closed her eyes tightly, and appeared to doze.

Then suddenly, as though someone had squeezed her, Pinky opened her eyes and her mouth and said, "Woe."

Curiously enough, at this very same moment Gracie waked up, wide awake, and lashed her tail back and forth frantically. Pinky noted that Gracie was sprawling on her stomach, her tail and hind legs in what might have been a springing position if she could have sprung at what she was looking at. But, as usual, she was headed toward the dusty little window under the eaves, and all she could do was have her tail give highly electric signals of almost unbearable desire.

Papa was doing a little typewriting, and Pinky, in an absentminded fashion, joined the game. This was to throw him off the track of what was really in her mind. Papa looked at the words on his typewriter. "Memo to myself: Must get up into the eaves *some* day," said the writing on the page.

Continuing with her game of throwing Papa off the track, Pinky again pretended to doze. And she purred to put him to sleep. Some games she loved playing with Papa. Others she preferred to play by herself, and the bold ascent to the eaves was to be her lone undertaking. When finally Papa seemed to be asleep, she leaped silently to the sand. Distracted momentarily by a little sand slug, she sat and observed its maneuvers, and you might think she had forgotten what she had set out to do. But Pinky never forgot what she set out to do, and if she stopped, it was mainly so her mind could contrive and connive. She suddenly pounced on the slug, ate it up, and resumed her slinky course across the sand.

She started to talk to herself as was her wont. "Now to find out what the old cat sees up there behind the window. No sand slugs, I bet, nor crickets, nor grasshoppers. They can be watched on the ground. Whatever it is, she is pretty excited about it. If that window were open, she'd be in there, bell or no bell, that's a cinch." We must remember that Pinky was granddaughter of a rather disreputable New York cat, thought to be Ash-can Sam, and sometimes her language was not as refined as it probably would become on longer life with the Pyes, all of whom were rather well brought up and had no disreputable grandfathers at all.

"And isn't it fortunate," Pinky continued to ruminate as she stopped to polish her paw for a moment, "that in the unusual excitement of having that new man in the house no one has thought to put on my collar and my bell?" This pink collar and bell were always removed at night so Pinky could not wake people up with her bell tinkling. Over the discussion of the eggs it had been forgotten.

She proceeded toward the little back porch, avoiding the front one, over which the two watchers, Gracie and Rachel, were perched. Gracie was still thumping her tail madly, and this made Rachel drop her *Green Fairy Book* to the ground and also made her turn around and lie beside Gracie, looking *in* for the first time.

Until now you may have thought that Pinky had some smart plan of getting up to the alcove under the eaves by way of the little roof over the small front porch, where Gracie always sits. You could not be blamed for thinking this, for you don't know about the mailbox. However, Pinky does.

Naturally on Fire Island there was no need for anyone to have a mailbox because no mail was ever delivered. Still, Mrs. A. A. Pulie, the lady who had built this cottage, had said, "Let there be mailboxes in front and in back in case anybody should call when I am out, so that they may leave a message for me or even half a cake or cookies if someone bakes them for me, a calling card, or anything."

So, beside the front door and underneath the little roof where Gracie and Rachel were staring wide-eyed through the porthole window, there was a perfectly ordinary mailbox painted green. And beside the back door there was another mailbox likewise painted green. But there the similarity ended, for this mailbox at the back of the house had a little door to it that swung either in or out, depending on which way it was being pushed, a little swinging door. And what do you expect was at the other, the inner end, of the little mailbox? Right. Another little swinging door that was cut right in the kitchen wall.

In this way the lady in the house, or whoever wanted to, could reach her hand inside the mailbox and get whatever was in it, the mail (if someday there should be delivery service), cookies, or anything, without having to go outside, not having to grab a shawl, say, to cover her head if it were raining or blustering.

And, in this interesting way, Pinky Pye had a secret passageway into the house and could come and go as she pleased. Pinky had planned this mailbox entrance for a long time, but she had been so busy with sparring, typing, and other games she had not had a minute until now to try it.

Getting into the house by way of the mailbox was not as simple as it sounds. But Pinky was a kitten of remarkable intelligence and skill, as clever for a cat as Ginger was for a dog. The reason it was no simple matter to get into the mailbox from outside and then out the other end and into the kitchen was that the lady who built this whole contraption had not really planned it for cats at all and there were no steps or runways leading up to it. The mailbox just jutted out from the weather-beaten shingle wall of the house.

But that was why going into the house by way of the mailbox was going to be so fascinating to a cat like Pinky, who was not the least bit interested in easy things. The harder the challenge, the happier she was. The whole Pye family had noticed this and frequently remarked admiringly upon her extraordinary imagination, persistence, and powers of observation.

In Pinky's mind she had it all plotted out, how she was going to do this great feat. She squatted on the ground a few feet from the mailbox. She wiggled her back end and she prepared herself for the leap. As surefooted as a miniature mountain gazelle, she leaped from the ground to the top of the mailbox. Now the really hard part, the amazing part comes, for how, from the top of the box, was she going to push open the little door and get in? It's too bad the lady, Mrs. A. A. Pulie, who had planned this fine mailbox, had not had a little piazza built on it as some birdhouses have. Then Pinky could have balanced herself on this piazza before pushing on in. But Mrs. Pulie hadn't, and after her nicely calculated leap, Pinky sat a moment on the top of the mailbox. She gave her head a little shake and cleaned her white paw, looking in its pale pink cushion as in a mirror, vainly, and giving the impression she often sought to give, of boredom. Actually she was taking in the whole surroundings, making certain Papa was still dozing and that there were no enemies around.

Then, carefully and slowly, Pinky accomplished a most miraculous feat, which would have stunned the family had they been around. Papa was still dozing, apparently, his hand over his eyes, and, except for Rachel, who, being on the other side of the house, couldn't see her, we know where the rest of the family was—off on safari.

But Papa wasn't dozing. He was watching Pinky through his fingers as she performed her miraculous feat. She leaned over the edge of the mailbox and pushed it open with her strong white paw. As it swung in, she crooked her paw inside the opening, getting a grip, leaned over, thrust her tiny head in, and, clinging fiercely to the rough inner surface of the mailbox, she crawled in upside down.

Not for naught was all her practice crawling upside down on the bottoms of couches and beds. In she went as neatly as if this were the right and usual way of going in houses. Furthermore, her tail did not get caught and embarrass her. Once inside she could have turned herself right side up, but she preferred not to; she preferred to crawl upside down to the back door of the mailbox, enjoying the sudden blackness after the glaring sunshine and scaring a

small spider that was likewise upside down beside her. When her head reached the back door, she did turn herself right side up, and she pushed this little swinging door open. She paused there, peeked into the kitchen, and appraised smells. In addition, she plotted the next leap.

Now the minute Pinky disappeared into the little mailbox, Papa, out of curiosity, hobbled over to the screened kitchen door to see if she were going to come out the other end or what, for she had never done this clever thing before and he was, quite understandably, impressed. So Papa was a witness to all that happened. He saw her bright little face poke out and survey the scene. And he saw her jump down from the mailbox to the kitchen table, and this leap sent the tablecloth like a flying carpet with herself on it to the very door of the living room. Pinky then sat in the middle of the tablecloth, looked around, shook her little head, said, "Woe," demurely, and cleaned her ear.

Pinky was a first-rate deceiver, and in case anyone were watching her (someone was—Papa—but her back was to him and she either was, or pretended to be, unaware of his presence), she wanted to imply that, well, now she was in the house and that was all she had in mind to do. However, to make the adventure as dangerous and interesting to herself as possible, she stopped cleaning her ear from time to time and peered about the room as though to intercept enemies. And she peered intently at the swinging door, entrance to the eaves, at the far end of which was the little window that so fascinated the great watcher, Gracie.

Pinky's tail gave an uncontrollable twitch as she contemplated that she, too, would soon know the secret of the eaves, which, so far, Gracie alone knew. Knowledge of whether the secret pertained to crickets, grasshoppers—or what—would soon be hers.

Through now with throwing people, whoever they might be, or onlookers of whatever sort, off guard,

Pinky sauntered into the living room, skirting the wall, and she hopped onto the living-room table. She sniffed Uncle Bennie's torn and empty cricket apartment house thoughtfully and she sniffed the new man's big cage and she pondered. She sniffed it again, butting her little nose against it several times, drawing back swiftly. Then stretching her neck and sniffing it again, she studied it; and then she pointed her nose into the air and she sniffed the air; then she pointed her nose to the eaves and sniffed again. The end of her tail gave a slight twitch.

Yawning, she surveyed the section of the house known as "in the eaves." This little enclosed section was built high up under a corner of the sharply pointed roof. It was supported by two sloping beams, and it had a swinging door that naturally was much larger than that of the mailbox, and this swinging door was built in two halves that met in the middle. In this little enclosed place behind the swinging doors Mrs. A. A. Pulie, the lady who owned and built this house, had formerly stored things—boxes, suitcases, old kelp, satiny driftwood, shells, and odd articles. Some of her things were still there, and the rest of the space the Pyes used for the same purpose, Papa having shoved some valises and boxes up there when they had arrived.

There wasn't any way of getting up to this loft except by stepladder, as Papa had, or by setting a chair on a table, as Rachel did when putting crickets' and grasshoppers' houses up there. That is, these were the only ways for humans. As for Pinky, she had studied this whole matter and she knew as well as if she had made this ascent a thousand times exactly what she was going to do.

A narrow beam wound around the walls of the cottage rather high up. On this ledge Mrs. Pulie had a display of plates and shells and driftwood, seaweed, framed pictures of winter sunsets from old calendars, and many other handsome objects. Pinky had no difficulty in leaping daintily to the mantel over the fireplace and from this to a fairly clear place on the ledging. She moved along this ledge with great care, and as she approached her journey's end, that is the closed swinging door, she paused to take stock. She sat on a crinkly piece of dried kelp that crackled when she moved and made her sneeze. She pretended not to notice Papa, whose nose was plastered to the screen door.

How different things looked from up here! It was a place for only a small kitten, however, for the narrow ledge became even narrower in front of the door to the eaves. A large cat such as Gracie could not balance up here, and that probably was the reason she had never tried; or else she was too old; or perhaps having had to wear a bell for so many years, she had lost interest in hard excursions, knowing that someone would be bound to hear her and put a stop to the venture, no matter what. As for Ginger, a dog, poor thing, he couldn't climb. Imagine his surprise someday when he should look up and should see her tail disappearing within!

Now. On with the journey. She edged her way to the middle of the ledge where the opening in the swinging doors was and . . . well, have you ever noticed how sometimes you have a very lucky day, everything seems mapped out in your favor? Well, so far, today was that sort of day for Pinky. The last time that Rachel had been up here she had apparently dropped a lollipop stick between the doors, and the little crack caused by this stick made a wedge for Pinky's paws. She stuck her paws in first, and then, squirming, wedging, nudging, bit by bit she squeezed between the two flimsy doors. And she got in!

Her heart pounded with pride and with delightful fear. The first thing that she took in was the sight of Rachel's face plastered against the dusty window, her eyes huge with astonishment. And then she saw the green, startled, jealous eyes of Gracie, who was moving her lips as though cracking something between her teeth.

Pinky stayed there with her back against the doors. Her tail wasn't even all the way in, for she knew the rule of making certain that a way of escape is assured, though she often disregarded this rule.

Too much safety foils adventuresome discovery. She now followed Gracie's glance, for after Gracie's first startled look of recognition of Pinky, without moving her head, Gracie had turned her big pale green eyes to the darkest corner of the eaves. Pinky stretched her neck, lowered her head, and peered in the same direction, and then at last she saw what it was that Gracie, the watcher, watched and what the watcher, Rachel, only a moment before had likewise discovered and was watching!

A bird!

All fluffed out, it looked huge to Pinky. And at the sight of Pinky, it made frantic efforts to fly, not away, but *at* Pinky. Its eyes were huge and round and fierce, and dragging a broken wing behind it, frowning, glowering, hissing, drooling for a taste of small and tender kitten, grown plump now on good Pye food, it rustled toward Pinky.

Pinky did not turn around. She backed out in a terrible hurry and, missing her footing, tumbled to the floor below.

Stunned, but pleased with herself, she swiftly recovered her poise. However, she decided to lose no time in getting back outside in the safe sunshine. She hopped to the kitchen table, squeezed herself back into the mailbox (the mailbox was right above the table, as you remember, so Mrs. Pulie doubtless could, while buttering herself a piece of toast, remove the mail, or whatever), and squeezed herself out again.

Jumping to the ground and crying, "Woe, o-woe," plaintively, she hopped onto Papa's lap, for he had hobbled back to his chair and was typing a wrong conclusion, which was that somehow or another, without any of them ever seeing her, Pinky had been accomplishing this amazing feat of going through the mailbox, ascending to the eaves, going inside, and eating up Uncle Bennie's crickets and grasshoppers.

This wrong conclusion was speedily righted by Rachel, who slid off the little roof and screamed, "Papa, Papa, guess what! Guess what!" She was so excited she could hardly talk. Finally she composed herself, stood before her father, rocked back and forth on her toes, and told him what she had discovered and that this discovery made her, at last, a bird man like him.

"Up there," she said. "In the eaves," she said, "is an owl, a tiny little real live owl! And I saw Pinky come in the door and look at him! He tried to get her and eat her up. He's the smallest owl I ever saw, a miniature!"

"My sainted aunt!" said Papa and, broken ankle or not, he hobbled indoors, put the stepladder in place, and up he went, to the eaves, to take a look for himself!

15

Follow the Dots

There, glaring fiercely at Papa from a dusky corner of the eaves, half hidden by a clump of dried kelp and with bits of it clinging to him, was a little owl. Now being a bird man of astuteness, it did not take Papa very long to realize that this little owl was the same little owl that Mr. Bish had lost in the gale off the coast of Fire Island. But it probably took him more seconds than it took you and me. It seemed incredible to Papa that that little owl could have been blown right into Papa's own house. But he studied the little owl thoughtfully, and in a flash this conclusion did hit him, that this little owl and the owl of H. Hiram Bish were one and the same. This was not the part of the world for pygmy owls, so this must be Mr. Bish's owl. The whole story tied together neatly.

"This," said Papa solemnly to Rachel, "is the owl of Hiram Bish!"

Rachel was astonished! She would have been happy to have discovered any owl in the eaves of the cottage called The Eyrie. But to have this owl, which she had discovered, turn out to be the lost-at-sea owl made her discovery even more important, and she danced up and down. "Just think how surprised Mr. Bish will be! And the zoo!" she exclaimed, helping Papa down. "Oh, why doesn't Mr. Bish come home. Why don't they all come home?"

Papa said they'd better leave the little owl up in the eaves, out of the cats' way (though they'd have to keep their eye on Pinky, make sure she didn't repeat her miraculous ascent and, next time, get him), but they'd better give him some food. By now Owlie

needed more than crickets and grasshoppers, Papa said. They found some chopped steak in the icebox. They put some of it on a dish, and this feast, along with a saucer of water, Rachel pushed into the eaves.

The owl hobbled toward Rachel so voraciously, she withdrew her hand in a hurry. "To think that all the times I put Uncle Bennie's grasshoppers up here, he's been up here too," she muttered. "And I never saw him! Well, he does look like that seaweed," she said to excuse herself. "But to think he must have eaten up all of Bennie's grasshoppers and crickets! But wasn't it lucky he landed in the house of a grasshopper collector?" she marveled.

"Well, the grasshoppers and crickets are what kept him alive," said Papa. "He's probably hurt and he hid all the time out of fear. No doubt, he came out of the kelp only for his nightly feast of grasshoppers."

"Well, I'm going up to the roof again," said Rachel, "and watch the owl and wait for the others to come back."

So up she climbed; and now there were two watchers on the little roof turned inward, she and Gracie. And back to his seat under the green umbrella hobbled Papa; and onto his lap hopped Pinky, still rather shaken from her perilous adventure.

What a relief, thought Pinky, *to be sitting here quietly on Pye's lap. Him, stroking my head behind the ears. Me, thinking and musing, my heart quieting down, my bravery refueling. I'll have to go back up there, kill that bird, and bring it down to Pye.* Pinky made a miniature crunching sound with her pretty mouth.

The afternoon sun was sinking, and soon the hikers to the sunken forest would be returning. Papa removed from his typewriter the sheet of paper on which he had reached his wrong conclusion about Pinky eating Uncle Bennie's eave crickets, and he crumpled it up and threw it away. Papa had a busy look about him as though he were going to do some very hard work. He lighted his pipe, but he speedily put it down in the ashtray and there it lay. Pinky enjoyed smelling the smoke and watching it waft out to sea. She sneezed appreciatively.

Pinky felt rested now, and she was resolved that if typing were going to be done, she was the one who was going to do it. Stretching, she sat up. She looked up at Papa and winked one eye. She frequently winked one eye at Papa or Rachel, giving the impression she was sharing a joke with them. Sometimes she winked both eyes, but this double wink implied boredom. Now she winked the one-eyed wink, and after it was winked she stretched herself and watched, like a superintendent, the inserting of a fresh piece of paper in the typewriter.

When all was ready, the paper in, the beautiful

blank paper that would soon be covered with little blank marks made by poking the enchanting disks, Pinky said, "Woe." Tentatively she pressed a key with her clean white paw. The joy, the bliss, of doing this! Soon the happy sound of clicking keys echoed in the clear and sparkling air.

Meditations of Pinky Pye III
Follow the Dots

You, my readers, who have been following my story, well know the ingenuity I exerted in order to get up to the eaves—the going in through the mailbox tunnel, the hopping onto the kitchen table, and the further dangerous and daring steps I took to wedge myself at last through the doors into the eaves. Because of Gracie's enraptured expressions, I expected to find more than crisp grasshoppers, true. A mouse perhaps. None of you, then, can imagine my terror when I found myself face-to-face at last with that which the old cat has been watching with such sharp attention.

And this is really what all of us watchers in this house have been watching, without knowing it, for one of us is always watching another of us. And this watching went like this, from one of us to another of us, and always ended up with Gracie, who was watching—?—in the eaves. Play this game of "Follow the Dots." It is on the next page. See? Now. Each dot represents a watcher. And each watcher is watching another watcher, and the last watcher, Gracie, is watching . . . well, follow the dots.

Now what do you have? Yes, an owl! Not a grasshopper or a cricket carefully caught by Uncle Bennie and stored up there, safe, he thought, from harm and danger. Not any of them! They have long since gone down into the stomach of that which was

The numbers are the watchers
Follow the dots

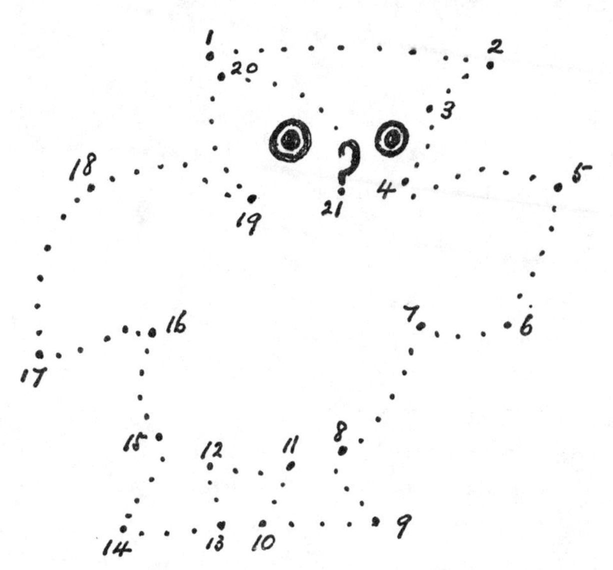

1. Uncle Bennie
is Watching
2. Grasshopper
who is watching
3. Uncle Bennie
who is watching
4. Cricket
Who is watching
5. Lady Bugs
who is watching
6. Jerry
Who is watching
7. Ginger
Who is watching
8. Jerry
Who is watching
9. Ginger

10. Mama
is watching a
watched pot
and

11. Papa
12. Pinky
Who is watching
13. Ginger
Who is watching
14. Uncle Bennie
and watching
15. and cricket
and
16. Papa
17. and Mama
and
18. Ginger
and
19. Rachel
Who is watching
20. Gracie
Who is watching

21. ?
in the
eaves

up there all along, a stowaway, an intruder in an orderly household, an unasked-for visitor without even a sleeping bag, a thing that probably wants to be a pet, to belong—an owl!

A small, immensely ferocious owl! Half starved on his prison diet of crickets and water, he wanted to eat me up! I foiled him, for I had the sense to retreat immediately. My nerves are still shaky, for I really was, for once, taken by surprise. It is quite a surprise to see an owl instead of a cricket. But I am going back. At the first opportunity I am going back. I shall push the door open a tiny crack, peek in, and watch that owl, see what he does up there by himself, study him. Then, when he is unsuspecting, dozing, I'll extend a paw within and swat him dead.

Plotting to trap me in the eaves, he bided his time up there, knowing that someday I would make the ascent. Well, I did make the astounding ascent, but any eating that is going to be done is going to be done by me, friend owl, not you. You will taste rather good, I imagine, after your special diet of grasshoppers. They have a molasses flavor that I have always enjoyed, and the combination of owl and grasshopper should be tasty. Like peanut-fed pigs, the flavor of which people rave about.

First to catch him though. I am working on the plan. Catch him, stun him, lay him at the feet of Rachel or Pye, the way the old harridan, Gracie, does her rats. She lays them at Mama's feet, tears open the stomach to make the eating easy. This is a story they never tire of telling. I tire of hearing it though. Boast, boast, boast. Brag. Substitute owl for rat and Pinky for Gracie, and we have a new and fresh family anecdote.

The sound of typing stopped. Papa looked at his watch. Four o'clock. Pinky tiredly settled herself along Papa's thin and lanky thigh and dozed. Papa half closed his eyes and half watched the roof watchers, Rachel and Gracie. Gracie still stared semi-alerted through the dusty windowpane that divided her from the glorious loot that was up there in the eaves.

"Incredible!" murmured Papa. "Incredible!" Impatiently he listened for the return of the picnickers. Then a smile came over his face. "Say, Rachel," he called up to his daughter. "When the others return, let's keep them in the dark for a while about the you-know-what in the eaves. OK?"

"OK," said Rachel a little reluctantly. She had wanted to shout it to them the minute she saw them coming. In fact, if she'd had a megaphone, she'd have been bellowing it out now. "Why?" she asked.

"We'll tell them at the right psychological moment," said Papa.

"All right, but may I do the telling?"

"Of course. You were the main discoverer. You're a real ornithologist."

Rachel hugged her knees happily. She got out her notebook to write down her first real bird observation of this summer. "What's the hard word for owls?" she called down to Papa. "You know, the genius word."

"Genus Strigiformes," said Papa.

"The pygmy owl of the Strigiformes is a great eater of grasshoppers," she wrote. "And crickets!!!!"

16

Meanwhile, Those on Safari

Meanwhile, how were things going with those who had taken the expedition to the sunken forest? Right now, the tide having receded again, they were on their way home. The sunken forest had been well worth the long and arduous tramp up the sands to it. From a distance it had looked like just a tangled web of boughs, or the tops only of trees, mainly holly trees and pines. But when you got near, you found that these tops of trees that you couldn't see the bottom of were the tops of real trees growing from a deep bowl in the earth.

"Wouldn't Rachel love this!" said Jerry. And, while Mama and Uncle Bennie waited on regular land, not sunken forest land, Jerry and Mr. Bish went down, down—exploring. At the boggy bottom of the forest Jerry had found an odd specimen of rock. He had not had rocks on his mind. Yet he had happened to glimpse this odd rock, which, upon careful scrutiny, turned out to be one he was not familiar with. Mr. Bish did not recognize it either. But then he knew more about birds than rocks. *This rock,* thought Jerry excitedly, *may be the very one that will tell the real and exact age of the earth and then we won't have to guess about that anymore at least.* He put this good rock in his wagon.

Now, loping wearily along the sand on their way home, the Pyes passed many fishermen in high boots, casting flies in the surf, hoping to catch a fish. They had been in the same places when the little safari had passed in the morning. Then, their faces had been bright and expectant, anticipating a fine

big catch on this wonderful day. The wind, they thought, was perfect. Now their faces were red and weary, and not one man they passed had caught one single fish, that is, not a fish that counted, for they couldn't keep the blowfish. Yet still they stood and cast their lines and still they hoped for a whopper. They had even eaten their sandwiches, those who remembered to eat, at the edge of the surf, holding their poles between their knees, not to miss a nibble. Their faces grew redder and redder. But they caught nothing.

"Don't they ever catch anything?" Jerry asked Mama.

"Poor things," she murmured.

After the first two or three fishermen had muttered, "Not biting today, wind's wrong," to the Pyes' friendly query, "How's it going?" the Pyes asked no one else. The lack of success of the real fishermen, however, made the extraordinary feat that Mr. Bish was about to perform even more startling. Mr. Bish was walking along the edge of the waves, trousers rolled up, barefooted, cooling his toes, when suddenly he caught sight of a huge fish flopping and floundering bewilderedly in the surf just a few feet out.

Without stopping to think, Mr. Bish strode right out into the ocean and with his two bare fists he picked up the large gasping, flapping fish. It was a perfectly good fish, not hurt at all. Probably it had been chased into shallow water by some larger fish. Mr. Bish said it was a sort of a herring and good to eat.

Imagine the expressions on the faces of the real fishermen! And imagine how the Pyes felt having a visitor visit them and just stoop down and catch a fish in that easy way! Just put his hands down in the water, he did, and had them come out with a fish that was almost two feet long and good to eat besides. His pants got a little wet, but that didn't matter. Jerry and Uncle Bennie were speechless with admiration, and Ginger barked happily at the ocean to express his enthusiasm. Mama, staying away from the fish's exuberant flaps, naturally was proud too. Mr. Bish was the envy of all the fishermen they passed who had not caught one single fish with all their paraphernalia and flies and bait and things, let alone with bare hands. Their hollow, bloodshot eyes followed Mr. Bish as he and the Pyes meandered up the beach toward home. The Pyes tried not to look boastful, but it is hard to conceal a two-foot fish, and though Mr. Bish was a modest man and was not flaunting his trophy, now and then he did give his fish a happy, jaunty swing.

When, tired and hungry, footsore and weary, the members of the expedition, with Uncle Bennie mounted like a charioteer atop their trappings and gear, trudged around the little cottage, they were spurred on by Rachel's enthusiastic greeting. "Papa, they're here. They're here!" And they revived sufficiently to recount the adventures of the day to the (they thought) lonely and bored injured stay-at-homes.

"Guess what! Guess what!" yelled Uncle Bennie while Pinky, sorry that the noisy fellow was back, flattened down her ears. "The man caught it in his hands, just his bare hands!" Pinky perked up and sniffed appreciatively.

Mr. Bish modestly displayed his catch. "Just luck," he said, shrugging. He had a pleased smile on his face nevertheless. "Just luck."

Mama went indoors to see about supper. "Cook the fish!" the children urged her. "Cook the wonderful fish!"

Ordinarily none of the children was fond of fish that had bones in it, but they were certainly going to eat this famous one. Mama did not like to prepare live fish, and this one still gave a gasp now and then. She prayed that when the time came to do something about it, it would not flip off the table. *If Mr. Bish had only caught a lobster that needs no beheading instead,* she thought wistfully.

"Don't you want to embalm this unusual fish and keep it on the wall over your mantel at home?" she called out to him. "You may never catch another."

Mr. Bish thought and then he said, no, he guessed not.

Mama opened the icebox to get out the lemon. Then she raced outdoors and demanded, "Where's my nice chopped steak that I was planning to have for supper?" Naturally, since all the family except Papa and Rachel had been at the sunken forest, one of them must know about the steak. "Did you give it to that spoiled cat?" she said, pointing to Pinky, who, not liking the tone of voice, hissed at her.

"No," said Papa truthfully.

"And we didn't eat it either," said Rachel. "We ate what you left in the wax paper for us."

"Well, where'd it go?" asked Mama bewilderedly. "Quite a lot of it is gone." And she went indoors to puzzle about the disappearance of the meat and try to get some sort of supper together.

Because the subject of the chopped steak had been brought up, Rachel thought that right now was a wonderful chance to break their astounding news of the day, which would make the fish story pale in comparison. "Papa, when can I tell them?" she whispered.

"You'll see," Papa whispered back. "I'll lead up to it. And give you the high sign when to tell."

Oh, thought Rachel. *That old "illogical" moment!* She could hardly bear to wait.

"Well," said Papa as they all, except Mama, settled themselves comfortably under the green umbrella, sipped lemonade, and relaxed. "What did you see on your walk today? And whom did you see at the beach? Any trace of your lost owl?" he asked his friend politely. "Great blow blow him into the sunken forest by any chance? Hear any to-whits, to-whos?"

Rachel was alerted. Soon the moment was bound to come when Papa would give her a nudge for her to say, "Guess who's up in our eaves?" She listened tensely for her cue. *It's like being in a play,* she thought. *And I have just one line to say.*

Mr. Bish started guiltily. "Why no-o-o," he drawled. "I knew there really was no hope of finding Owlie. But I suppose I still hoped against hope that I might find him. I confess I even whistled for him now and then, his pygmy owl call, you know." Mr. Bish gave a profound sigh.

Jerry said, "I learned the call too. Listen." And Jerry gave his version of the call of a pygmy owl. This struck Uncle Bennie funny, and he laughed so hard no one, no one but Papa, Rachel, Pinky, and Gracie, that is, sharers of the secret of the eaves, heard a very faint echo of this call from inside the cottage. Rachel and Papa exchanged knowing looks. And so did the big and little cats. Rachel signaled her father, "Now? Now?" He shook his head. "Not quite now," his lips formed the words.

Shucks, thought Rachel.

It was so nice out nobody wanted to go indoors to eat, so they had supper on a little table under the green umbrella. Mama was the quickest cook in the world and the best. That's what they all said. Here she had thought they wouldn't have anything for supper, what with most of the chopped steak gone; yet they had a wonderful supper, a delicious sort of stew made out of the remainder of the meat, some canned kidney beans, tomatoes, and rice. They also had fresh corn on the cob, cucumbers, and tomatoes. In addition, as an appetizer, they had the hand-caught fish. All took one taste of this in order to be able to say that they had eaten Mr. Bish's fish that he had caught bare-handed without even a bent pin to help. No one liked it. But still it was a splendid thing to have done, to have caught it in this unusual fashion, whether anyone liked the taste or not.

At one point, while dishes were being brought into the kitchen, Rachel and her father happened to be alone. "Oh why, why can't we tell them now?" she wailed. "The suspense is terrible."

"I think they should all rest a little while, relax, allow their suppers to digest," said Papa. "After all, they have had a strenuous day hiking, delving down into sunken forests, catching a great fish. Besides," Papa added, giving Rachel a little wink, "I want to build up to it. Have a little fun first."

"All right," sighed Rachel. She still thought there was no time like the present. (How right she was, you shall presently hear.)

Now the others came bearing the dessert, the coffee, and the peaches. The men lighted their pipes, sat back on their beach chairs, hands behind their heads, and puffed away. Mama said the dishes could wait, and everybody but Rachel relaxed. It began to grow dusky and, inside, the one little flickering kerosene lamp cast a warm and golden reflection on the sand. There was a little talk of this and of that, and then it seemed that Papa simply could not keep off the subject of owls, a delicate and painful one, surely, for their guest, thought Mama.

And even though Rachel knew the story was going to come out all right in the end, that, as in most good stories, there was to be a happy reunion, still she could not help but squirm along with the others. In fact, she was tempted to whisper in Mr. Bish's ear, "Don't worry. You'll soon have your owl. Just as soon as Papa has had his old joke." Of course she could not do this, since poor Papa had to have some fun once in a while, even if he did have a broken ankle.

"Now, Bish," said Papa. "If the high wind that

tore your owl from the hands of your wife as she braved the storm on the deck of the SS *Pennsylvania* on that fearsome and epochal night had blown him, by some freakish chance, to some very safe and protected place, would you say that he might have stayed alive? That he might, in fact, still be alive on this very night, as we sit here, exactly two weeks to the dot since the night of the great blow? Eh?"

Mr. Bish was a thoughtful-looking man. He had some scars on his chin that the children took to be the result of battle wounds. ("Verdun," Jerry had said to Rachel. "Yes," she had answered.) These scars added to the thoughtfulness of his face. He gave Papa a long and respectful scrutiny, for no bird man likes to give a wrong answer to another bird man, and he drew in his lower lip and bit on it. Then he gave his reply.

"Pye," he said, "I think I have to conclude that my owl, beneficent landing or not, has perished. He had no idea how to find food for himself."

"Well," said Papa (and here Rachel wondered if her cue were coming now and wiggled her bare toes in nervousness), "I have heard of American birds, a robin, for instance, being blown across the ocean to England and remaining alive."

"Yes," agreed Mr. Bish. "I have heard of that and also of the opposite happening, of a widgeon recently being blown from England and fitting in nicely in

America. But as I say, Myra and I caught Owlie when he was a baby, and unlike that robin and that widgeon he has no idea how to protect himself or find food."

"If your little owl were able to find his own food," said Papa, "what sort of food does he like to eat?"

Goodness, thought Mama. *Edgar is awfully gay and happy tonight considering the morbidity of the subject under discussion.*

"Grasshoppers," said Mr Bish. "Grasshoppers, praying mantises, crickets . . . and he likes good red meat, or a juicy little mouse, a lizard. He used often to settle for good old plain chopped steak."

"Oh-h-h," said Uncle Bennie. "Grasshoppers and crickets. Tonight you might hear my crickets sing."

"Uncle Bennie," said Papa. "I doubt if your crickets will ever sing."

"They will too," said Uncle Bennie. "They ain't all ladies." His eyes strayed up to the little porthole window. So did Rachel's. Rather absentmindedly, for she was so absorbed in not missing her cue if Papa would ever give it to her, Rachel noted that Gracie was not up on the little roof where she usually sat.

Pinky was not around either. It seemed odd not to have the cats watching and playing in their usual places. But Rachel did not have time to ponder about this, for Papa was going on and, sensing a mounting excitement in his voice, Rachel became even more on the alert than ever.

Papa was saying, "I know it must be hard to talk about your dear pet owl, and it must be especially hard to recall his song, his call. But you have made your owl so real to us, almost like a pet of the Pyes' in fact, that I know I, for one, feel very close to him. It would be a great treat to all of us for you to do as you did this afternoon at the sunken forest, imitate little Owlie's special call. Please do call him as you used to do back home in Alta Vista."

Mama shuddered at what she thought was Papa's lack of tactfulness. If his foot had not been broken, she would have given it a kick the way she did when he forgot to listen to deaf Mrs. Price. This was not the man who had knocked her down on the escalator and then married her. This was a mean and cruel man.

But after one glance of surprise at his host Mr. Bish complied. He wetted his lips. Then first he gave the call of the pygmy owl, a long series of bell-like notes that he steadily and regularly repeated. Then he gave its song—a short quaver, then a pause, and then three bell-like notes.

The night air was clear, and when Mr. Bish stopped, a silence fell on the group, a sad silence because he must miss Owlie so. Rachel almost forgot that Owlie wasn't missing after all anymore, and she whisked away a tear. In that silence, as a far distant echo, faintly came the same call that they had just heard Mr. Bish give—a long series of bell-like notes, repeated often and steadily, exactly the same call. But it stopped suddenly—in the middle of a note. Mr. Bish leaped to his feet, looking bewilderedly about.

"It's your owl!" cried Rachel, not waiting for cues any longer. "It's your wonderful little owl!"

At this moment from inside the cottage there came a great crash!

"Oh! My sainted aunts! The cats!" yelled Papa. "Come on, all of you, or Owlie will be a goner after all!"

Into the cottage they all raced, the lame-footed people going faster than the surefooted ones.

The little doors of the mailbox were swaying... swaying....

Mr. Bish was so confused he didn't know what to do, where to look.

Gracie was obviously responsible for the big crash. She had knocked over an urn of seaweed that had been on the ledge near the swinging doors of the alcove. Her anxious, startled eyes were pale and glassy green and they were fastened on Pinky. For once, the big cat was watching the little cat instead of the other way around.

Pinky was sitting on the narrow ledge outside the swinging doors. She was holding up her little white paw and looking at it and shaking it. "Woe," she said when she saw the family.

"How long have those cats been in here?" asked Papa.

"Oh-woe," was all the answer he got, and he got that from Pinky. She shook her paw as though to rid it of something.

"Oh-h-h," groaned Rachel.

Was Owlie inside of Pinky?

17

The Secret of the Eaves

The great question in the minds of Rachel and Papa, the others being completely puzzled and in the dark, was—had the cats been in the eaves and hurt the owl, perhaps even eaten him, while Rachel and Papa had been lolling outside creating psychological moments?

Only a moment before, however, they had heard the little owl hoarsely answer the call of Mr. Bish. Could he possibly have been killed in the brief moment that had elapsed since then? They could not be sure. Hemmed in as he may have been by two cats, one big and the other little, who knows what may have happened? His hoarse call may have been a call for help. He had certainly stopped suddenly in the middle of a note as, oh heavens, Uncle Bennie's crickets used to stop in the middle of chirps.

Rachel was already up on the table, advancing to the eaves. "Go away," she said sternly to Pinky, giving her a push and a swat and sending her sprawling.

Oh-woe, thought Pinky on the floor. Her tail waved angrily. *The way people come along and take the credit!* she thought.

"Come on up, Mr. Bish!" said Rachel. "Help! Your Owlie's up here." And then she prayed, "Oh, let there be a nice compact alive little Owlie and not just a pile of feathers."

Still bewildered but as quick to help now as he had been when yanking the great herring out of the water, Mr. Bish bounded onto the table, took his flashlight out of his pocket, pushed open the swinging doors, and then . . .

"Owlie!" he exclaimed. "Owlie!" His voice broke. And forgetting that his wife was in Washington, he said, "Myra! Owlie's here!"

He whistled pygmy owl tunes as he used to do in Alta Vista, and the little bird, covered with bits of dry seaweed, fluttered to him like a baby bird just learning to hop. Tenderly Mr. Bish picked him up. "He's wounded," he said. "His wing is wounded. But otherwise he seems fine."

Pinky was now adjusted to the fact that things had not gone as she had planned. She sat on the hearth with an approving expression and nodded her head and cleaned her ears. She was trying to deceive the family into thinking that she had meant all along to be merely a guide, divulging the secret of the eaves to them.

Gracie, banished into the night, sat on the windowsill and peered in, looking sullen. Obviously she had been foiled in her attempt to get into the little storage room. Being too big for the very narrow ledge, she had awkwardly knocked over the heavy urn in her greedy haste to beat Pinky to the prize.

"Do you want this?" asked Jerry, handing Mr. Bish his owl cage.

"You bet I do!" said Mr. Bish, and he put Owlie in it right away.

Owlie did not mind. For a while he glared wild-eyed and accusingly straight ahead of him, as though

he were just barely restraining his anger and tears. Then, feathers all ruffled up, he cowered in a corner of his cage and fell to brooding and scowling.

Now they all adjourned, owl, people, cats and dog, to the green umbrella, where, under the star-studded sky, they could mull over this whole unusual series of events and piece them all together.

"Well . . . well . . ." said Mr. Bish hesitantly.

An awful thought struck Rachel. Did Mr. Bish have the idea that the Pye children had known all along about this owl in the eaves and that they had grown so fond of him they were hiding him in case he should turn out to be, as indeed he had, Mr. Bish's own West Coast owl named Owlie?

Somehow Rachel felt guilty. Taking grasshoppers, Gracie the watcher, Pinky, and all other things into consideration, it seemed incredible now that the Pyes had not known all along about Owlie being up in the eaves. Rachel was relieved when Papa, who sensed there might be a misunderstanding of this kind, said, "Bish. Today, while you sunken-forest hikers were away, our kitten, Pinky, got into the house in a very unusual way, that is, through the mailbox, which has little swinging doors to it. Curious to see what this clever little creature was going to do next, I hobbled to the screen door and watched.

"She then, by a roundabout and challenging route along the ledges, arrived at the eaves, which have swinging doors too. Assuming that she was after Uncle Bennie's grasshoppers, I gave the matter little more thought other than to marvel at the cleverness and ingenuity of this kitten."

"M-m-m?" said Mr. Bish.

"It was Rachel," Papa went on, "who, practically at the same moment as Pinky, made the discovery of the presence of your little owl. Rachel had wondered what our other brilliant cat, Gracie, always watched as she sat watching on the little roof over the porch, eyes glued to the little porthole window. At first she had assumed as I had... grasshoppers. But Rachel, a true scientist, taking nothing for granted, ferreted out what it was that Gracie watched. So today, from her place on the hot little roof, with foot throbbing..."

"Oh, Papa," remonstrated Rachel, pleased nevertheless with the glory.

"She has the making of an ornithologist," said Mr. Bish with solemn conviction.

"She is one, she already is one," agreed Papa.

"Oh, I just wondered why Gracie watched and watched," said Rachel modestly. "Anybody would have done the same."

"But, Pye, why in Sam Hill didn't you tell us about Owlie the minute we came home this afternoon?" asked Mr. Bish with a shade of quite understandable annoyance in his voice.

Papa looked a little sheepish. After all, he had almost waited too long. But Mr. Bish accepted his apologies amiably and his explanation, which was that he had wanted to lead up to the climax, Mr. Bish's call, hoping Owlie would answer and stun Mr. Bish with joy and surprise. And this Owlie had done.

"He sure stopped in a hurry at the approach of cats," said Mr. Bish. "But what I wonder, too, is how Owlie got up there in the first place?"

"I know! I know!" said Rachel, speaking tensely. "I have it figured out. He was blown in through the little round porthole window the night of the big blow. Because when we moved here, that little window was open and Mrs. A. A. Pulie said to be sure to close it; but we forgot to close it until the night of the big storm. By the time we closed it Owlie had already been blown in. Mama was afraid bats might blow in! "

"Ugh!" said Mama, glad it was an owl and not a bat. "Why didn't that owl ever sing so we could hear him? Oh . . . those rustlings . . . That was Owlie all along!"

"Uh-huh," said Mr. Bish. "As for singing, he would be too terrified. Or he may have injured his throat the famous night he got blown in. Imagine Owlie being blown into the very best place that he could have been blown into on the whole East Coast! Blown from one bird man to another. All wrong the saying, 'East is East, and West is West, and never the twain shall meet.'"

Mr. Bish was fond of serious remarks of this sort, and the children puzzled the meaning of the sayings silently and politely.

"The odyssey of an owl," murmured Mr. Bish, still dazed over his good fortune. He then softly sang more owl songs to Owlie while mulling over the facts of the case. "But what did he eat all that time?" he asked, interrupting himself in the middle of a song. "Aside from his wing, which is broken, he seems in good shape. And what did he drink? After all he has to have food and water."

"That's the most wonderful thing of all," said Rachel ecstatically. "Don't you see? He ate crickets and grasshoppers. All Uncle Bennie's pets that are named Sam. That's what he ate. We'd put them in the eaves every night and every morning they'd be gone. We kept wondering and wondering what was happening to them."

When all this about Uncle Bennie's pets and the red-threaded one and the blue-threaded one was explained to Mr. Bish, he nearly fell over backward.

"Owlie is the exception that proves the rule," he said. And he slapped his knee again.

It'll get black and blue, thought Uncle Bennie.

"What exception? What rule?" asked Rachel.

She thought the owl was famous enough already without further distinctions.

"Well . . ." said Mr. Bish. "I have never heard of a little owl that was captured in infancy and hand-fed ever since being able to stay alive if he were suddenly set free. Even with crickets placed as temptingly close as Uncle Bennie's were, I would have thought it impossible for a hand-fed owl to have the sense to tear open cricket boxes, however flimsy . . ."

"Weren't flimsy," interrupted Uncle Bennie. "Were strong cricket houses."

"M-m-m," said Mr. Bish. "Strong cricket houses is what I meant. To get the crickets out of the strong cricket houses and then to eat them up! Extraordinary. More and more extraordinary."

Papa and Mr. Bish then exchanged a few remarks concerning birds, in difficult language. Owlie blinked sternly and proudly at Uncle Bennie, who frowned back at him whether he was an exception to an owl rule or not.

Mr. Bish continued to marvel at the unique string of circumstances that had blown his owl off the SS *Pennsylvania,* over part of the ocean, and through a porthole window of the renowned Edgar Pye's cottage named The Eyrie. And to think that then, unbeknownst to any of the Pyes, Owlie had been fed a very special and fine diet of pet crickets and grasshoppers belonging to the youngest, though an uncle, member of the family; and that at last he had been discovered by a smart little girl of the age of nine and the name of Rachel.

Now of all these interested and excited people Uncle Bennie alone looked sad and far from ecstatic. In fact, he looked the way he always looked when he was just barely able to hold back his sobs. Finally, brokenly, he said, "All my pets, my pets named Sam. The owl ate them up. They were fine until the owl blew in."

For a moment everyone was silent. Thoughtlessly no one had realized the gloom into which, naturally, this answer to Uncle Bennie's question of the last two weeks—what happens to my crickets?—would cast him.

"They was all going to sing to you tonight," said Uncle Bennie. "I thought they had a plan and was all gathering in a eave to sing, like a choir."

Rachel was the first to hit on a way out of the misery. "Just think, Uncle Bennie," she said. "Just think. Your nice little crickets kept this famous owl, who has been in the newspapers, alive for two weeks. And this famous owl is going to be in a zoo where everyone can go and see him. And everyone will remember that if it wasn't for you no one would know what this sort of little owlie looks like because he would be dead. You kept him alive."

Uncle Bennie looked long at the owl, who scowled back at him. The owl said, "Who, who!"

"He's thanking me," said Uncle Bennie, feeling a little better. "They're dead and he's alive. That's fair, isn't it?"

Uncle Bennie began to take more and more interest in the little owl, who frowned at him, unblinking and stern. It was as though his crickets had turned into an owl. "You know," he said to himself. "Things do change into other things, they do."

"The whole series of extraordinary events must be written up for *The Ornithologist*," said Mr. Bish, slapping his knee. "You must do it, Pye."

Papa gave a slight cough. "It will be written up," he said. "But not for *The Ornithologist.*" And he would say no more even though beseeched.

"So that's where my chopped steak went today," said Mama, glad to have light on that subject, which had continued to baffle her. She was glad also that her husband had not turned into a mean man, just a teasing one.

Owlie made an attempt to say something. "Sounds more like a raven," said Mama.

"I think his voice will come back," said Mr. Bish, "now that he is over his fright. But he better sleep in the eaves again tonight, in his cage, safe from cats and dog."

In the dusk they could see Gracie, up on her

little roof again, body turned inward as usual, from habit; but her face was looking grimly down at Owlie. "It's a wonder that big old cat didn't try before tonight to get up to the alcove, since she has apparently known about Owlie all along," said Mr. Bish.

"Gave up trying to catch birds years ago," said Papa, "with that bell. She contents herself with watching and crunching, pretending she's eating a bird. But Pinky may try and get up to the eaves again."

"Well, Owlie will be in his cage, so owl can't eat kitten and kitten can't eat owl," said Mr. Bish.

Pinky cast a winning, wistful, sad glance at them. Then she swung by her two front paws from a rung of a chair. Mr. Bish had become very interested in Pinky. He thought her mailbox entrance and her ascent to the eaves fabulous. A description of the string bean game that Mama had given him this afternoon while on safari piqued his curiosity, and he said he wished he could see this played. Pinky was in a good mood for the string bean game because what Mama termed "night madness" in cats and children had overtaken her. She first leaped wildly after a little moth and then she leaped from one lap to another. Next she crawled upside down on the underneath side of Mr. Bish's canvas chair. Mr. Bish yelled, "Ouch!" and jumped up, so it was a good time to go indoors.

Rachel played the string bean game with Pinky, which caused Mr. Bish to marvel, for he had never before seen the like of it. After this Pinky settled down on Rachel's cot and winked one eye at Rachel. Pinky was practicing the deception of being through for the night. But those who knew Pinky best, Papa and Rachel, were not taken in. The tip of Pinky's tail gave a twitch as she saw Mr. Bish shove his owl cage with Owlie in it up into the eaves.

"Oh-woe," said Pinky quietly.

Mama said it was time to call in "the old cat," which, since the advent of Pinky, was how everyone now referred to Gracie. So she went to the back door and mee-owed. Mama knew better than to say, "Here kitty, kitty, kitty," when she wanted a cat to come in. Most cats never come in to that old tune. They just play the game of "Take Your Time." Mama knew you have to mee-ow to get a cat in, and the more variations you have practiced, the more effective your call will be. "Cats come bounding in to a good mee-ow," Mama turned to explain to Mr. Bish, who was unaccustomed to the idea. "At least mother cats or cats that have ever been a mother, and Gracie has (what a mother! someday I'll tell you), will come bounding in. See?"

For Gracie had come bounding in at the third loud mee-ow.

Papa said he didn't know what the neighbors in the next cottage, The Dunes, thought of all this mee-owing. In Cranbury people were used to Mama's mee-owing. Mama said the people in The Dunes wouldn't think, with all the cats and pets over here, anything at all about her mee-owing.

Gracie hopped on Mama's lap and looked up anxiously in Mama's face. "She's never quite sure about the mee-ows, whether I do them or not," explained Mama, and stroked Gracie's thick fur coat. Then she told Gracie what a smart cat she had been with all her watching. Gracie purred at the praise. She did love Mama, at least, which was something in her favor.

"Didn't I tell you that Gracie might lead you to a bird discovery, not necessarily a puffin, but an important bird discovery?" Mama said. "And you wanted to leave her home!" she said reproachfully to Papa. "Where would Owlie be now but for Gracie? Still up in the eaves and undiscovered," she said. "That's where Owlie'd be!"

Pinky did not like the conversation. Who had made the original and famous ascent to the eaves? Gracie? Ho! No. No one but Pinky Pye. That's who.

18

A Speech in a Sleeping Bag

Here I am at last, in a sleeping bag at last, thought Rachel, happily wiggling her toes in the soft warm coziness of it. She had been worried for fear she would not have a chance to sleep in the sleeping bag, but she had. When it was time for bed, Uncle Bennie had said, "Who's going to sleep in the sleeping bag tonight? I'm not."

And Jerry had spoken up hastily, before Mr. Bish could reply, and said, "Well, me and Uncle Bennie had our chance last night. It's not fair for us to have the sleeping bag every night." You would think that Jerry had slept in the sleeping bag sixteen times, he spoke with such fervor.

Rachel could hardly stand the suspense. Of course Mr. Bish would want to sleep in his own sleeping bag, having missed out on it last night. But how she wished he would let her. It would probably be her last chance to sleep in a sleeping bag until she was old enough to go on far bird trips with her father, not easy ones like Fire Island. Rather timidly, while Mr. Bish was thinking up his answer, she said, "I would like to sleep in the sleeping bag if it's all right with you. That is, if you are not too tired to sleep in a regular old bed like my cot after that long trip you took today to the sunken forest and catching that big fish and getting your owl back."

Mr. Bish smiled graciously and said, "All right, Rachel. You may sleep in the sleeping bag."

"Oh, thanks," breathed Rachel ecstatically.

Mama smothered a sigh. She would much rather have her children sleeping in beds than in sleeping bags or any other sort of rough-and-tumble contraptions. But she was a perfect hostess, and a guest, she thought, should be in a bed and not on the floor, so she agreed.

Then Uncle Bennie had the idea it would be nice to sleep in a cardboard crate. He became very busy putting bears' blankets in it and a small pillow. He was quite angry when Mama firmly put her foot down against this move. But once he was back in his own bumpy little beach cot again, he was happy to be there. He had had one heroic night in a sleeping bag and that was enough.

"Rachel," he said.

Rachel turned her glowing face to him. "Yes?" she said.

"Did you mean it when you said I am a hero because of my crickets?"

"Yes, I did. Ni-ite."

"Nite."

Uncle Bennie lay on his cot half asleep, half awake, watching as much as he could of other people's preparations for going to bed, a pleasant and restful thing to do. He had been a hero three times in his life now, he told himself. This may not sound like a lot of times, but to have been a hero three times when you are only four is a very good record. Many people go through their whole lives and are never a hero. That's what Rachel had said. The first time he had been a hero was because he was an uncle. The second time was in May when he had recognized Ginger, who had been lost for such a long time, and coaxed him home to the Pyes' house. And the third time was today, saving the life of a little owl by feeding him his best pets.

"Good night, Owlie," he called. "Good night, crickets," he added, for old time's sake.

Papa said, "We better barricade those swinging doors. Here, Bish," he said, handing him the dictionary. "Put this in front of them, will you? We don't want Pinky, whose middle name is Persistence, paying a night call on that owl of yours, sticking her sharp little claws into his cage. I have a hunch she is plotting a further exploration of the eaves." Papa and Pinky exchanged glances of mutual esteem.

"Pinky Persistence Pye. That sounds like a Puritan name," said Rachel.

Then Papa hobbled over, leaned down, and gave Rachel a good-night kiss. "Well, how's life in a sleeping bag?" he asked. "How's our little ornithologist?"

"Fine," said Rachel. She closed her eyes and prepared to make a speech to herself, her favorite way of going to sleep.

Jerry looked at Rachel. He could see her very well from his narrow cot. She looked blissful. *She*

feels the way I did last night when I first crawled into the sleeping bag, he said to himself. He continued to watch her, and the look of radiance on her face did not fade. She didn't begin to toss and turn and try to find comfortable positions between the knobs on the floor of knotty pine. *She really is loving it,* thought Jerry, growing envious. *I bet sleeping in sleeping bags really is wonderful. I should have tried it again. It probably takes one night to get used to a sleeping bag and after that you probably never want to sleep in anything else. Boys, that is, not girls. Girls probably haven't the sense to feel the knobs the first night. Look at Rachel! Just look at her!*

A look of glory was on Rachel's face.

"People . . ." Rachel began her speech, which she was giving in Pythian Hall in Cranbury to a cheering audience of famed ornithologists and also family and friends in the front rows. "Birdaceous friends . . ." she said. "Thank you for giving me this nice medal for discovering the owl. By rights this medal should be cut in four parts because there were three other members of the Pye menage (menagerie, Papa says that's short for) who helped with the discovering—Uncle Bennie, Gracie, and Pinky. They're three and I make four. Four pieces of 'pie.' Pie, Pye. Get it?

"It may seem odd to have an owl blown off a ship in a howling wind and zoom right into the tiny porthole window of our cottage called The Eyrie, which means a place for owls. Why not the cottage next door called The Dunes? Fate. Happenstance. But once Mama, that's my mother . . ." (Here Rachel glanced at Mama, who, in the front row, was brushing away the tears as fast as they fell. Mama was weeping, not because the owl had been blown in by fate, but because Rachel was making such a wonderful speech.) "Well, once Mama had a hard bug zoom right into her ear. She was standing in the open window of Papa's study. And this bug happened to zoom right straight into her ear like a bullet. She had to go to the doctor to have it out.

"So. That's two things that got blown into small places and shows that more often than you think, things do zoom into small places not knowing or being able to help where they zoom. And there is no need for astonishment.

"And so, here I am at last, in a sleeping bag at last." (Rachel was growing sleepy and she forgot she was in Pythian Hall addressing the ornithologists and not on the floor of The Eyrie in a sleeping bag.) ". . . O-o-oh! What was that?"

"O-o-oh! What was that?" was not part of Rachel's speech in Pythian Hall. They were real words spoken out loud because there had been a big bang and a terrible, heavy thud.

Everybody else waked up and yelled, "Hey! What was that?"

"Just the dictionary," said Papa calmly, and lighted a lamp.

There sat Pinky on the ledge cleaning her paw. Owlie gave a hoarse but really loud cry. It was much louder than the call he had given at dinnertime in answer to Mr. Bish's call.

"By jiminy!" exclaimed Mr. Bish joyously. "His voice is coming back!" Since Mr. Bish was of the type that rarely shouts with joy or anger and who seldom shows surprise even when pulling a large live fish out of the water with his bare hands, you can imagine how very joyous he must have been feeling to have raised his voice so loudly now that people in The Dunes must surely have heard him. It showed how very much he wanted to have Owlie restored to health and singing happily again.

Pinky had been a little unnerved at the bang, which had exceeded her expectations. But she was pleased with herself and the attention. "Woe," she cried, and leaped through the air, as though after butterflies, right onto Rachel's odd bed. She closed one eye. Mr. Bish was wedging a newspaper between the swinging doors, making them close together more tightly. "Now, pussy, you stay out!" he said sternly.

Pinky looked up there innocently. *As if I couldn't get that out if I wanted to,* she thought. *Tomorrow . . .*

Rachel began, "People . . ." It was her speech again. "People . . ." and off she went to sleep. Usually her speeches did put her to sleep.

19

Farewell and Hail to Owlie!

Owlie was going away now. There he was in his cage in H. Hiram Bish's hands, staring fiercely at those on land as the little boat he was on started putting out to sea. Mr. Bish had plopped his popular sleeping bag on the floor of the boat, which was the little one, the *Maid of the Bay,* and also his one valise. With one hand he held up the little owl cage so owl and Pyes might view each other as long as possible; and with the other hand, he waved. Mr. Bish was smiling. He certainly was a happier man departing than he had been arriving, reflected Rachel. There he had been, three days ago, the one man on the ferryboat, alone and with an empty cage; and in his heart little hope of finding his owl, his rare and splendid owl. And now look at him, a happy beam on his face, his owl in its cage, and his sleeping bag beside him.

It would be hard to tell what Owlie was thinking. He certainly must have a great distaste for boats, having had his terrible and calamitous adventure when on one. "You'll soon be in the zoo," Rachel called to Owlie. But then, to Rachel, this seemed such a sad place for little Owlie to wind up in, she had to brush away a tear.

He is famous though, Rachel reassured herself. *He will, next to that great old bear they have there, be the most looked-at specimen in the zoo. That should be some comfort to him. And he may be happier being with a lot of other rara avisses: than being a lone bird pet in someone's house. All the same I wish he were ours. Yes, I do. Owl Pye. What a nice name! Owlie Pye.*

All of the Pyes, including Papa, who, in his wheelchair, cheerfully rang his bell if he saw a person even a block away, had gone to the wharf to wave good-bye to their guests—the man guest and the owl guest. They hadn't known for certain that Mr. Bish was going today; but just a few minutes before it was time for the boat to depart he had said, well, he guessed he better be on his way. He scooped up his valise, which he had never unpacked, and his sleeping bag and Owlie in his cage, and he and all the Pyes rushed to the boat, which he just barely made. So there he went, he and his pet, putting out into the Great South Bay, the Pyes' first and only guest on Fire Island. This departing made the entire family feel sad, deserted, and lonely.

"I want my mother, my own mother," said Uncle Bennie. "Not *your* mother, Rachel, who is my sister, but my own real right regular mother," he said. "I wish I had gone on the boat, too." He pushed his big sister, Lucy Pye, *their* mother, away from him because he was not interested in huggings from anybody but his own real right mother just then. "And all my crickets is gone!" he added.

"Well," said Mama. "Your mama's coming soon for a real nice visit, and maybe she'll stay until it's time for us to go home; and your papa is coming too for his week's vacation. So don't be sad."

"I want them now," said Uncle Bennie. He sat on a wooden pile and, through tears, looked at the bright green silky seaweed clinging to it. He swung his short legs and he put his thumb in his mouth. Then in a second he pulled it out. "Hey!" he yelled, forgetting his misery and his face reflecting the bright morning sunshine rippling on the waves. "Hey, you know what?"

"That's what," said Jerry, who could never resist this awful joke.

"You know what?... Stop it, Jerry. Don't say it again, that's what..." said Uncle Bennie, speaking so fast Jerry couldn't get the "that's what" in. "You know what? I haven't sucked my thumb since tomorrow."

Uncle Bennie frequently mixed up yesterday with tomorrow. But they all knew what he meant and exclaimed with pride and joy over such an achievement.

"Good boy!" they said, and they had to hug him because it was such a hard thing to do, give up sucking a thumb. Uncle Bennie didn't mind being hugged now and hugged back, so that he almost fell into the bay.

"That's fine, that's fine," said Mama. "But get away from the water, will you? Please?"

"Oh, I won't fall in," said Uncle Bennie. "You don't need to worry." But he got up anyway and sat in

Jerry's taxi and studied his thumb. It had quite a callus on it from bygone days when he used to suck it.

"I broke the habit," he said happily and out loud. And he began to suck it again. "Just to see how it used to taste," he said. "Like when I was little I used to suck it all the time. Remember?"

"That was just yesterday," said Jerry.

"Yes," said Uncle Bennie happily, filled with ecstatic wonder at himself.

Jerry was balancing a long thin mahogany-stained bamboo stick first on the tip end of a finger and then, being successful with this, on the end of his nose. He was walking along the top of the seawall, while the wagon boys cheered. Papa said for him please to get off the seawall while balancing a long thin stick on his nose.

"Oh, I won't fall in," said Jerry.

"I'm sure you won't," said Papa. "But you just might."

So Jerry moved to a safer area to balance his thin pole on his nose. The twins in their peppermint-striped suits passed by, looked a moment, not knowing whether to cheer or to imply they saw nothing unusual in this sort of balancing. Deciding on the latter, "We can do that too," they said primly, and climbed into the wagon beside Uncle Bennie.

Meanwhile, the little boat with Owlie and the

bird man was putting fast across the bay. The Pyes could still see it, could in fact still distinguish their tall friend, Mr. Bish. Seagulls were following the *Maid of the Bay* and so shall we for a moment, leaving the Pyes watching from the wharf

Mr. Bish had placed Owlie in his cage on the seat in the stern of the boat. Although the *Maid of the Bay* was not a fishing boat, the seagulls showed an amazing amount of interest in it. They swooped and fluttered unpleasantly close, alarming some of the passengers, who put newspapers over their heads. Even though he was an expert bird man, Mr. Bish did not fancy seagulls this close to him. It had not dawned on him, as it has on you, that the seagulls were curious about the little owl.

Flapping their wings wildly and screaming in their frightening way, two gulls in particular circled about Mr. Bish. "What's the matter with you?" said Mr. Bish. "Shoo!" he said. "I haven't any fish." He wondered if he still smelled like that herring. He waved his arms to frighten off the gulls. One gave a sudden low swoop, picked Mr. Bish's owl cage up in his long orange beak, and away he flew with it.

This story might have had a very sad ending if the gentle wind had not been blowing in the right direction. It *was* blowing in the right direction for a happy ending though, for the gull glided in on the wind with his trophy in his beak, right to the very lap of Mr. Pye, who, in his wheelchair, was so overwhelmed at the amazing nature of this bird feat that it was a moment before he remembered to brandish his cane, ring his bell, bellow, and frighten the owl thief. "Wha-hoo, wha-hoo!" he said, which seemed to do the trick, for the gull flew away. Then all the Pyes, speechless with wonder and incredulity, crowded around.

The owl was lying on its back in its cage, claws in the air, stunned with fright.

"My!" said Papa. "My sainted aunt! The poor little tyke! He has had his share of extraordinary adventures. It will be a wonder if he is still alive."

He was alive though. Gradually Owlie revived, stretched one thin leg and then the other, and soon cowered in a corner of his cage, glowering fiercely and looking terribly anxious.

At this moment the little boat putt-putted back to the dock. Mr. Bish, in the name of the Department of Zoos of the United States of America, had demanded that the boat be turned around and that it pursue the seagull that had stolen the owl, property of the government. This the captain grumpily did while the passengers cheered. When the *Maid of the Bay* pulled into port, Mr. Bish stepped ashore and for the second time in two days was reunited with his owl.

"It looks as though this owl wants to belong to the Pyes," said Mr. Bish. "But a promise is a promise, and to the zoo he must go."

Mama had on a dark blue shawl, and she gave this to Mr. Bish to wrap around the cage so that no more seagulls would see the owl and be tempted to swoop off with him again, and also to enable the poor little thing to have a quiet moment of sleep or rest, if he could. It was a wonder he had not died of heart failure.

So, again good-byes were waved, kisses blown, and the little boat putted doubly fast across the bay to make up for lost time. Mr. Bish hugged the cage to him so that nothing of any alarming nature, not wind, not gull, could swoop his owl away again.

"Phew!" said Jerry. "What a thing that was!" He and the others sat down on the seawall to make comments and exchange notes about what they had seen of the swooping gulls and the stealing of the owl by one of them and his long and graceful glide to Papa's very lap!

"Well!" said Papa. "In all my long life with birds, during which I have heard, read, and observed many curious things about them, this theft of an owl in its cage by a seagull tops all."

Then Papa said he had some work to do and that he had taken enough time off, so he started for home, leaving his family still gaping after the *Maid of the*

Bay until it had disappeared altogether. They were not certain that some other miracle might not happen and they did not want to miss it.

Pinky, who had been safely ensconced in Papa's coat pocket and firmly held there during the swoop of the gull, was now allowed the freedom of the ground. She gamboled along behind Papa, looking so adorable Rachel gasped, "Oh, look at her! Look at her! Did you ever see such a cunning cat. There's something about her face! Oh, her face! That little pointed chin! And she has such a busy little brain, as though some plan is going on in it all the time."

"I know it," said Mama, hoping the plan would not involve the slices of liver she had left on the kitchen table, seasoned and ready to cook for lunch. "Don't let Pinky in the house," she called after Papa. But Papa didn't hear her and Mama had forgotten about the mailbox entrance.

Peeking out from between Papa's firm, restraining fingers, Pinky had seen the departure of the owl, so she knew that *that* owl was gone. But could she be sure that there wasn't another owl up in the eaves, maybe a whole flock of them, small and young and tender? "Where there's smoke there's fire," she said with amazing sagacity for such a small kitten.

The rest of the Pyes, lingering behind, were still trying to spot the very seagull that had snatched the cage from the boat and deposited it at their feet.

They thought this seagull must know them even if they didn't know him. It was uncanny to think one of these glistening, waxy, cold-eyed, cold-looking, ominous-sounding birds was a friend of theirs. A flock of them was lined up on the top of the boathouse roof, and all of them were staring in the same direction, excepting one. This wrong-way gull might be their friend. Instead of looking upon the owl-snatcher as a thief, they now looked upon him as a friend, since he knew them.

"Well," they gasped. "Well! Phew!" They began to get ready to go home.

Rachel's foot, which had been swollen with flea-bites the day of the discovery—goodness, was that only yesterday?—was still quite swollen.

"You will have to stay off that foot," Mama said to her.

"All right," said Rachel reluctantly. Now that the great bird discovery had been made, there was not very much to do, just sitting still. *Oh, I know,* she said to herself, for she was the kind of girl who always had a million plans in her head, things to do, to make, or just to think about. She could work on her bird scrapbook, she reflected as they all started home for lunch.

A good lunch, thought Mama, *and easy to prepare, the liver being seasoned and ready for the pan.*

Alas! Just as the Pyes opened the kitchen door,

who should shoot out of the inside of the mailbox but Pinky Pye! She landed skillfully on the table all right, but she slid on the liver, slithering it and the paper it was on off onto the floor. There it lay all peppered and salted and covered with flour. Gracie, edging in on Mama's heels, took in the situation at a glance and immediately took charge. She grabbed the liver and ran under the stove with it, growling fiercely like a tiger. It was a long time before anyone could get it away from her and then who wanted it anyway?

"Oh, my," said Mama. "Let them have it, let the cats have it."

So the cats got all the liver, and this taught Mama never to leave anything on the kitchen table again, not with that mailbox entrance available to little Pinky; and Mama had to fix hot dogs and baked beans for lunch instead. This was very good though, so everybody, cats and people and dog, the cats having to surrender one slice of their trophy to Ginger, had a good lunch.

The next morning Rachel and Uncle Bennie could hardly wait to get down to the wharf to meet the early boat. Each had a reason of his own. Uncle Bennie, having been told that his real right mother was coming to pay a visit soon, intended to meet every single boat from now on. His mother was probably going to try to surprise him and not tell anyone on what boat she was going to be. And he was going to surprise her and be at the boat no matter what one she was on.

Rachel was interested in the boats that brought over the newspapers, the morning *Times*, the evening *World*. Jerry pulled her to the wharf in his taxi so she could stay off her foot as Mama had said to do. Rachel thought it was not likely that there would be something in the paper so soon about the owl, but it was possible. And sure enough! There was a long story!

Mr. Bish must have been met in the Pennsylvania Railroad Station by newspapermen, who had then worked all night to get this story written. There it was, right on the front page of the *Times*, with a picture of Mr. Bish and Owlie taken in the railroad station. RARE LITTLE OWL FOUND, said the big headlines. Under the picture it said, "Little owl lost at sea not lost after all." Rachel began the story: "The little daughter of the famed ornithologist, Mr. Edgar Pye, must be given credit for locating the owl of another ornithologist, Mr. H. Hiram Bish."

Heart pounding and unable to continue to read without the entire family around her, she demanded she be taxied home and never mind the customer that Jerry might miss—let Touhy Tomlinson have him.

It was quite a long account. All gathered around to catch a glimpse.

"Get out of my way, Janet," said one twin, for the twins had been at the cottage watching Pinky type. "Let me see!" said Joanne.

There it was! The entire thing, bringing in how the little owl had been blown out of Mrs. Bish's hands on the deck of the SS *Pennsylvania* on the night of the great wind, July the fifth. The account of the watching of Rachel Pye and the cat Gracie was very dramatic; and much was made of Uncle Bennie's pet crickets and grasshoppers, which had saved the life of the owl. There was even something of Pinky's ascent to the eaves, but this they got wrong, so it's lucky that Pinky and Mr. Pye had it all set down right on the typewriter or we might have had it wrong too. The paper said she had been tucked up in the eaves, accidentally, in a sleeping bag! It's lucky we know the truth—the mailbox end of it. And the story did not mention the fish of Mr. Bish, but then why should it? This was not a fish story, it was an owl story.

Rachel cut the story out and pasted it in her scrapbook and impatiently awaited the next day. Her father suggested that she also get the *Washington Post* and see if there was something in it, since the owl was headed for the nation's capital. This paper had to be ordered especially for the Pyes, and it would come a day late. When it came, however, there it was again, practically the same story as had been in the *Times* but with a new picture of the little owl in his new habitat, the zoo, looking as ruffled, fierce, and dismayed as ever.

"Poor little thing!" said Rachel with a lump in her throat. "He really doesn't want to be in a zoo. I bet he was really glad when that seagull brought him back to us. Maybe he signaled the gull to do that."

"He'll get to like it there," said Papa, "with all the other birds. After all, he has never known what it is to be free!"

"Except for that wild ride on the wind!" said Rachel. "That must have been wonderful for him, even if he was scared."

Still Rachel couldn't help crying over all the animals locked up in zoos; and the next day's papers didn't help her to feel better, for there was a picture of the little owl moping in a corner of his cage, his wing in a splint, not mingling with the other birds, not happy at all.

On the next day there was a small story down in the corner that said it was feared the little owl, the zoo's latest acquisition, might not live. It was possible, the paper said, that the owl had had more hardships than it could stand. ("Misses my crickets," said Uncle Bennie gloomily.) The paper also said that the donor of the little owl was very worried and he had asked for but had not yet received permission to take the owl away again, for a short time at least, and try to nurse it back to health.

The next day there was no story in the newspaper nor the next nor the next nor for several more. But one day about a week later there was a story saying that Mr. Bish had been given permission to take his ailing owl back from the Washington zoo and try to restore its health.

The next day when Rachel went with Uncle Bennie to meet the boat, it was already putt-putting into sight and someone was frantically waving from the deck. Since this was the early boat and had few passengers, there happened to be no one meeting it except Rachel and Bennie, so the person must be waving to them. They waved back.

"Do you see that person waving?" asked Uncle Bennie. "Well, I think it is my mother."

Rachel thought it looked like a longer, skinnier person, but she could not tell, for the sun dazzled her eyes.

The person wasn't Uncle Bennie's mother. As the boat swung around and came into the shade of the dock, they could see who it was. It was Mr. H. Hiram Bish. And in his arms, what did they see? Little Owlie in his cage looking as bright and healthy and fierce as he had after his two weeks of special diet of Uncle Bennie's champion crickets and grasshoppers.

Mr. Bish had a beseeching expression on his face. He smiled apologetically and said, "Is your father home?"

They went to The Eyrie, and Gracie, from her lookout on top of the roof, saw the scene enacted below of the return of the man and the bird.

Papa was dozing under the green umbrella. But Mama, who was hanging up clothes, dropped the bag of clothespins, took out two that were in her mouth, and greeted their recent guest warmly. She noted that he did not have his sleeping bag with him.

The owl gave a call. His voice had improved during his stay at the zoo at any rate, and he no longer sounded like a hoarse raven. Papa waked up with a start. "My sainted aunt!" he said, hopping up. He grasped Mr. Bish's hands cordially. He had taken in the situation at a glance, and he knew, probably as well as you and I do, what request was about to be made of him and the Pye family. Out it came.

"Well," said Mr. Bish. "There are some pets that pine away if they are put in zoos, and I am afraid that mine is one of that sort. He has more sentiment than I thought. I am afraid, and the zoo people agree with me, that his life will be very short if I leave him there. So, what better place to leave him than with my brother ornithologist, Mr. Edgar Pye, and his bird, cricket, cat, and dog loving family."

"We could keep him in the eaves again," said Rachel. "He wasn't any trouble last time."

"We have two cats, you know, and a dog," said Mama. "Once Ginger killed a chicken." But Mama knew what the outcome was going to be. She and her family were about to have still another pet, and the name of this pet was going to be Owlie Pye. She saw it coming and said nothing else. After all, she had as soft a heart as the rest of her family and didn't want it to be said of her that she had let a little owl die in a zoo when it might have lived if she hadn't said, "No."

What she said was, "It is destiny... And I suppose we can put a board across the door into the eaves and keep the cats out."

"Yes, and in Cranbury, he can stay up in Papa's owl eyrie. Since we call Papa's study the Eyrie, it is good to have a live owl in it or what is the sense of the name?" asked Rachel.

"What, indeed!" agreed Papa.

"Well, anyway," said Uncle Bennie. "He is not going to keep on eating my grasshoppers and crickets, that's one thing he ain't."

"Of course not," agreed Mr. Bish. "I'll leave a chopped meat fund for him."

Pinky sat on the sand at their feet. She was looking up at the owl and he was looking down at her.

Their eyes were equally round. Pinky made a slight crunching sound.

"No, no," said Rachel. "This owlie is now a member of the family."

"Woe," said Pinky.

And then Mr. Bish, who could not even stay for lunch he was in such a hurry to get on with his expedition, dashed for the boat, which had already given its second toot, leaving the Pyes to make what adjustment they could with his beloved little owl, whom they decided to keep on calling just "Owlie."

"We have Ginger, Owlie, and Pinky Pye," said Rachel.

"G.O.P.," said Papa with a faint chuckle.

"What does that mean?" asked Uncle Bennie.

"Grand old party," said Papa.

"Where's the party?" asked Uncle Bennie. "Where's the cake?"

Well, life settled down fairly normally again for the Pyes. Gracie was happy to have the owl back in the eaves. It added zest and youth to her life to have something to watch again as she basked in the blazing sunshine. And it was interesting to watch Pinky's energetic attempts to open up the little door, which was too well barricaded with a stout board for her to succeed.

Occasionally Papa took the owl in his cage out for fresh air and a ride in his wheelchair. This attracted so much attention Papa said it was too bad he couldn't charge for the show. He really could have charged for the show, what with a sparring and typewriting cat, famous already all over the island, and now with a famous owl who had been written up even in the international press. Some Frenchman, an acquaintance of Mr. Pye's, had sent him a clipping of the story of the owl, the wind, the crickets and all from a Parisian newspaper; and if you don't think that it is exciting to see yourself written up in a French newspaper, then you must be the sort whom nothing excites. It certainly looked very important in Rachel's book of clippings. The Pyes took to calling Uncle Bennie, *l'oncle Benné*, for a while, the way it was in the French paper.

Then life settled down into its regular channel, with picnics and beaching, and the children were very bronzed from the sun except for Rachel, who only freckled; and the grandmother and the grandfather arrived and had to be shown the sights, including the sunken forest and the spot where the famous fish was caught bare-handed. And then summer was over and the days were growing short and all their hearts turned to Cranbury again.

20

At Home Again, on the Little Balcony Again

Now the Pyes were home again, in Cranbury; and Rachel and Jerry were sitting on the little square upstairs veranda. A gentle breeze swayed the branches of the giant elm tree that stood beside their tall and narrow house. It was evening and darkness came early now. The Cranbury crickets were singing, and these crickets had a clearer, quicker note than those Fire Island crickets, what was left of them at any rate after Uncle Bennie's catching and Owlie's eating of them.

The return trip had been so arduous that a separate book could be written about it. Have you ever tried to travel a great distance in an old Ford that was given to blowouts (for Sam Doody, their High School Senior friend, had come and got them) with a dog, a little cat, a big cat, and an owl in a cage? I hope not. However, their good friend Sam Doody, even though he was very very tired from the trip and from hearing "The Owl and the Pussycat" recited many, many times, said, "Well, neither of the cats had kittens and that's something, isn't it?" But then he was a senior in school, captain of the football team, and the duster of the church, and he was never upset by anything.

So here the Pyes were then, at home, and hardly able to realize that they had had a vacation at all.

"The first day of vacation is long. The rest is short," said Rachel.

They had come back yesterday, and it seemed as though vacation was a sandwich.

"It's a sandwich," Rachel explained to Jerry. "Life in Cranbury before we went is one slice of bread. Life in Cranbury after coming home is the other slice of bread. And the vacation on Fire Island is the inside of the sandwich."

"Which is better, which is more important?" asked Jerry, hoping to get Rachel into a "which is more important" game. "The bread or the inside of the sandwich?"

"The bread, naturally," said Rachel. "But you wouldn't have a sandwich without the inside. You'd have two slices of bread. So it's all important if you want to call it a sandwich."

"Does it seem to you as though we had a vacation? How long have we been back?" asked Jerry.

"Since yesterday. But it seems as though we have been back forever. It seems as though we never went," said Rachel. "Except of course we know we went," she said hastily lest Jerry think she was a nut and, worse still, call her one as he did sometimes. "We know we went because now we have Pinky Pye and up in the Eyrie we have Owlie Pye."

Ginger was at Jerry's feet and he was resting happily. Pinky was in Rachel's lap and purring so hard her little body was shaking. Papa was standing in the doorway, behind the children, taking slow puffs on his pipe. Then he turned away quietly and went upstairs to his study. In a corner of this room where there used to be only a big old stuffed screech owl, there was now also a real little owl, Owlie Pye. They frequently stared at each other, the real owl and the stuffed owl.

When the little owl saw Papa, he hopped off his perch and marched to the door of his cage for a stroke and a scratch on the head, which he liked although throughout this show of affection his expression remained frowning and fierce.

"Can't help his looks," said Rachel. "He's awfully cute, anyway."

How were Pinky and Gracie getting along with this new member of the family? When the owl in his cage was permitted downstairs, the cats hugged the walls. The owl and they scrutinized each other constantly, the owl turning around as on a pivot whenever a cat slinkily circled around him. The cats were not given an opportunity to tear open Owlie's cage, and Papa was having a hardier one made of very strong wire so that it would be impossible for them or even for mountain lions to tear it apart. So Owlie was assured of a pleasant, yet just dangerous enough, sort of life ahead; and his presence lent spice to the lives of the cats, who could always imagine how good he would taste if they could only taste him.

Pretty soon the sound of Papa's typewriter could be heard busily clicking in the night air. Pinky pricked up her ears. Should she stay here and purr on Rachel's lap or go upstairs and help with the typing? Unable to decide, she polished her paw. Mama was busily scraping the dinner dishes downstairs and of course Uncle Bennie was back in his real right home with his real right mother and father. The house seemed empty without him.

"Can you believe it?" said Jerry. "School starts tomorrow. Book reports, physiology..."

"Physiology! Will you have physiology now?" asked Rachel, who was one year behind Jerry in school.

"Yop. Physiology and all kinds of things, even harder things," said Jerry.

Rachel gently scratched Pinky behind the ears. Pinky soon had enough of this. She shook her head, stretched, yawned, and jumped down. Crying "Woe," she walked into the house. In the doorway they could see her little black outline as she stood listening, white paw raised.

"She hears Papa typing and she wants to do some herself," said Rachel.

"Yop," said Jerry.

"Now isn't it funny?" said Rachel. "All the while that Papa was sitting under the green army umbrella typing, he was not writing about birds at all. He was writing about a cat. This is a secret but it's true. Don't tell anyone," said Rachel.

"How do you know?" asked Jerry.

"I found it out that day when you and Mama and the bird man and Uncle Bennie left me and Papa at home, the day I discovered Owlie."

"But how?"

"I happened to glance, just out of curiosity, at Papa's paper and it was about a cat. It was written as though a cat had written it. A lot of it was in the 'I' person."

"I don't mind 'I' books anymore," said Jerry. "But I tell you what I do mind, and that's book reports. Do you like book reports?" he asked Rachel.

"Well," said Rachel, "I like books but I'm not crazy about book reports."

"There are four things about book reports that I don't mind," said Jerry. "Name of book, name of author, setting, and time. Those four things. I hate moral, meaning, and plot."

"Names of characters is not bad either," said Rachel.

"Yes, but then you have to say whether good or bad," said Jerry.

"Yes, but that's not so hard," said Rachel.

Jerry got back to the subject of Papa and Pinky and their typewriting. "Suppose that that book that Papa or Pinky, or whoever it is, is writing, supposing we should get it from the library someday and have to write a book report on it?"

"Yes, imagine writing a book report on your own cat!"

Pinky was still standing in the doorway, listening. She looked at them as though she thought they were both nuts, and then she bounded up the stairs to the little eyrie. She leaped onto Papa's lap, watched the keys hop up and hop down, and then she thought it was her turn and so she typed.

"Let's go and look over Papa's shoulder," suggested Jerry.

"Oh, no," said Rachel, aghast. "He doesn't like that, you know. He never has liked that."

"I know," said Jerry rather reluctantly. "But I should like to see some of the words coming out of the mind and onto the paper. Well, anyway, it's nice right here. My, it's nice to be home again, isn't it!"

"M-m-m," said Rachel. "That tree. And that star! And smell it, smell the air, just smell it."

They both smelled the air and then they continued with their conversation. Is there anything pleasanter than to sit in the evening time on a little porch under a large and rustling tree and talk with your brother? Rachel wondered. And no one calling anyone nuts.

EPILOGUE

Yet, after all, Jerry and Rachel had not been able to resist going upstairs to the little eyrie. Their eyes nearly popped out as they saw the following words hopping onto the paper.

BOOK REPORT
by
Pinky Pye
on the book called *Meditations of Pinky Pye*

Name of book: Meditations of Pinky Pye.

Author: I wrote it. Pye put in the commas.

Setting: No setting. Since a book is not exactly an egg, no setting on it was necessary.

Time: A very good time.

Characters: Pinky, ah-h. That's myself. A good character.
Pye, the man. That's him. A good character, good at games.
Typewriter. That's this. A good character.
Gracie. That's her. An old New York cat. A shady character.
Ginger Pye. A dog here. A noisy character and bad.
Bugs. Good characters.
Uncle Bennie. A lively boy in charge of the bugs. A shady character.

? in the eaves. A shady character.
Owlie. A shady character.
Pye, the lady. A cook. A good character.
Rachel Pye. A girl. A watcher. A good character.
Jerry Pye. A boy. A shady character and noisy.
Birds. Shady characters. To be caught.
Grasshoppers. Shady characters.
Peepers. Noisy and shady characters.
String beans. Good characters.
A girl with red hair. A catcher of kittens in crab nets. A shady character.
A man named Bish. A clever catcher of fish. But a stealer of my bird. A shady character.

Describe three of *these characters briefly:*

a. *Ginger Pye.* Ginger Pye is a jealous, noisy, stubborn, greedy, foolhardy, pathetic, untidy dog.
b. *Gracie Pye.* Gracie Pye is a mean old cat. She is a talented watcher, however, and a brilliant mouser (they say). She is a spiteful, jealous creature, but she is neat and quiet.
c. *Pinky Pye.* Pinky Pye, ah-h, is the main character of the book, the "I" of the book. In this description, out of modesty, I'll refer to myself as "she," not to have I, I, I every minute. She is brilliant, charming, beautiful, winning, brave, clever, cute, wonderful, irresistible, and full of ingenuity. She has a sweet nature, loving, spirited, and gay. She is inquisitive. She has unlocked screens in windows and exited. She is a keen observer and a great watcher, and she made *the ascent to the eaves.* She is adorable, lovable, enchanting, and fascinating. A whole book could be written about her and has been. Look in the library for it. Don't skip a word of it, it is all true.

Tell what the plot is, enough to show that you have read it:
The plot is this: There was I, Pinky, living in the reeds and the rushes in that other land across the waters. There were peepers to catch, grasshoppers, too; minnows to watch and my reflection in the salty pools; the dew in the morning to drink, my brother to box with; butterflies, ten to a dozen. Then one day along with my sisters and brother I was caught in a crab net by a girl with red hair. Where are my brother and sisters now? It is not in the plot of this book to tell, for I am the plot. A good character, Mr. Edgar Pye, and his girl, Rachel Pye, rescued me from the bad character with her nets and contraptions. Liking them, I took up residence with them. In this household everyone is a watcher of some sort. Some are better than others. What is in the eaves is the main thread of this story, and in the end I reveal the secret. Gracie is apt to boast that she knew it all along. Old cats are boastful. Don't listen to her. As though you'd have a chance! She can't type.

Tell what the style is:
The book is written in the latest style. When the man, Pye, does the typing, the style is wordy. When I do the typing, there are plenty of interesting dots and dashes and exclamation points and the going is swifter. Do not skip the parts that the Pye man writes, however, for they are not bad, being mainly about me. I prefer to use this sign ($) instead of the exclamation point (!), but the Pye man always erases it. It looks greedy, he says. I think it's prettier though.

Criticism: (This means tell what is good or bad about the book. And if you like it.) Yes, I like it. It is too short, that's all.

Climax: (This means the most exciting part.) As though I have to tell you—The Ascent to the Eaves, of course.

Illustrations: Excellent, though they do flatter Ginger.

Moral: The moral is, watch and you shall be rewarded.

Comments: I have heard of one cat already who is named after me, Pinky Pye Cohen. There will probably be others, and to them all I send greetings. Since I caught, or rather led to the discovery of the you-know-what up in the eaves, I am as famous as the dog here named Ginger Pye. I, too, got my picture in the paper, though Ginger had to horn in of course. It is in the *Cranbury Chronicle* for yesterday.

"$#&?*-"

This is the way that Pinky wrote "good-bye." Some cats do speak and type in different languages, you know.

The mouths of Jerry and Rachel Pye were hanging open. They were speechless, foreseeing, as they did, a new era in book reports.

"Well," said Papa, "since we have finished with the book and we have finished with the book report, what do we do now, Pinky Pye?"

Pinky cast a slurring glance at the little owl, and she made a slinky exit. At the door she looked back at Mr. Pye and then, for a long and thoughtful time, at the owl. "Woe," she replied sadly.

Eleanor Estes (1906–1988) grew up in West Haven, Connecticut, which she renamed Cranbury for her classic stories about the Moffat and Pye families. A children's librarian for many years, she launched her writing career with the publication of *The Moffats* in 1941. Two of her outstanding books about the Moffats—*Rufus M.* and *The Middle Moffat*—were awarded Newbery Honors, as was her short novel *The Hundred Dresses.* She won the Newbery Medal for *Ginger Pye.*